SPIRIT OF DEFIANCE

SPIRIT OF DEFIANCE

Wallis Peel

CHIVERS

British Library Cataloguing in Publication Data available

This Large Print edition published by BBC Audiobooks Ltd, Bath, 2008.
Published by arrangement with the author.

U.K. Hardcover ISBN 978 1 408 41231 2
U.K. Softcover ISBN 978 1 408 4 1232 9

Printed and bound in Great Britain by
Antony Rowe Ltd., Chippenham, Wiltshire

For Bill and Hazel Shepherd

All the main historical events in this story took place but I have used a writer's licence to alter dates and times slightly for the benefit of the story.

The historians do not appear to agree as to exactly where P Ostorius Scapula died nor from where he conducted the campaign. It is fact though that he was, for a time, the commanding officer at the Roman Fort above today's Chipping Sodbury, South Gloucestershire, as well as being Governor of Britain.

It is also uncertain exactly when men first entered Britain with the Christ story but come they certainly did. Until then it was the Druidic faith that held sway and respect among the tribes.

*   *   *

During the first half of the first century Britain was held by many tribes whose territory roughly corresponds with the places below:-

Dumnoni	Cornwall
Durotriges	Dorset
Belgae	Parts of Somerset and Wiltshire
Regni	Southern England
Cantii	South-east Kent

Atrebates	Wiltshire
Dubonnii	Gloucestershire, the Severn Valley
Catuvellauni	Thames Valley northwards
Iceni	Norfolk
Silures	South Wales
Ordovices	North Wales
Cornavii	North Midlands to Lincoln
Brigantes	Lancashire and Yorkshire
Demeytae	Dyfed
Trinovantes	Essex
Deceangli	Old Flintshire
Caledones	North Scotland
Sewlgovae	South Scotland
Dorini	North Ireland
Vulunti	North Ireland
Menapii	South-east Ireland

Everywhere had Roman and British names but to avoid confusion I have, where possible, used modern ones.

ONE

Jodocca knew she had started to flush, and broke eye contact, apparently to study the nearest tree's leaves. There had been a light shower in the night and tiny droplets twinkled in the early morning sun. Concentrating hard, she tried to control rising guilt.

Macha gave one of her favourite sniffs. 'That was an excellent trading report, daughter,' she began, 'but I still find it hard to understand why you spent so long away and allowed the pack train to return without you and, more to the point, rode back without a bodyguard?'

'I told you!' Jodocca protested just a little too quickly. 'A horse kicked him and broke his leg. So we had to stay behind. Anyhow, you know perfectly well I am a trained and skilled fighter. I don't need a bodyguard!'

Macha's probing gaze became cynical. There was more to this than met the eye. Jodocca stood like a little girl caught in the middle of doing something forbidden. Macha opened her mouth to berate her, then suddenly changed tack. Jodocca would only get stubborn if bullied. It was high time she married again and started breeding. It was a crying shame that her husband had been killed in a boar hunt and there had been no child.

1

'It's time you married again,' she began smoothly. 'Now why don't you—?'

Jodocca faced her. 'No!' she snapped, realising she was being rude. After all, her mother was in her mid-thirties, and old. So she softened her voice a little. 'You and my dead father arranged the last marriage and what did he turn out to be? Useless!' She ended scornfully, 'Anyhow at twenty, I've been adult for years, and I'll do my own matchmaking now, thank you, Mother!'

They squared up to each other, their resemblance obvious with the same very fair hair, fine features, and widely spaced blue eyes under high foreheads. They had square jaws, straight noses and generous faces, though Macha's now held crease lines.

Jodocca was not beautiful and knew it. Her attraction came from a fierce spirit and strong character, inherited from her long-dead father, a chief, who had been able to command instant attention without moving a muscle. Jodocca knew she had the same ability, which she used ruthlessly.

Macha could smell a secret. 'But what were you doing,' she persisted, 'for a whole week?'

Jodocca shrugged. 'Just looking around,' she said, and realised how thin this sounded. 'Colchester is a marvellous little town,' she added, brightening, with cheeks glowing pink. 'Do you know, Mother, it has a large defensive earthworks, a large ditched enclosure and a wonderful system of tracks. And the trade! There was a temple there too and—'

'Roman!' Macha snorted.

Jodocca's face held out a gentle smile now. 'There is also a wonderful way to get clean. The Romans are far ahead of us that way.'

Macha was unimpressed. 'Dirt never harmed anyone. It keeps the skin warm in winter,' she snapped with rising irritation.

Jodocca eyed her patiently. 'Maybe,' she replied slowly, 'but I've seen many small battle wounds on dirty arms and legs, which turned nasty and fatal. I have often wondered if dirt had something to do with this. Anyhow, I was able to explore everywhere; because there are so many tribes' people there, I was able to be just another Briton with them,' she ended as memories tangled together. 'I tried a bath with some women,' she said, then wished she could have withdrawn the words.

'How could you? A Briton? Since when have Romans let Britons in their precious baths?'

Now Jodocca floundered. 'I met someone who arranged it,' she said hastily.

'Who?' Macha demanded to know. Surely her suspicions could not be correct? Not her daughter?

Jodocca eyed her squarely. 'Someone with whom I think I may have fallen in love. We had a whole week together and—' She

3

flinched at the ice in her own mother's eyes.

'A Roman!' Macha accused. 'That is it, isn't it? How could you? How dare you? Your father must be turning in his grave!'

'You married for love. You told me so. Why can't I too?' Jodocca shot back hotly.

'A Roman is the enemy, that's why, girl! Use your head a little!' Macha was appalled, and she attacked again. 'What do you think the tribe will think of you? Going over to the enemy! They are stealing our land. Look at the fool tribes who have agreed to become clients of Rome. Effete Britons aping the Romans. My own daughter, and I—' and words left her temporarily.

Jodocca struggled to defend herself. 'Some of the tribes are not at all sorry to see the Catuvellaunian hegemony merged under the Romans.'

'Not us Dubonnii!' Macha shot back, then she took a deep breath. A row would get her nowhere. 'You had better tell me all about it,' she ended with a sigh. Though, what good could come of this was beyond her.

'He trod on my foot,' Jodocca said softly, and a rare warmth filled her eyes.

'Eh?'

She nodded at her mother. 'I was studying a piece of pottery and he accidentally trod on my foot, apologised, then looked into my eyes,' she paused, remembering what she had felt. Brown eyes, the colour of an autumn nut,

4

had held her gaze while his huge height and breadth were overpowering. From him came something magnetic and Jodocca knew she had stood there, flat-footed, lost for words, as she had felt something eerie flow between them.

'Who are you?' she had whispered, rooted to the spot while people milled about them, trading, talking and eyeing the wonders of Roman building.

'Marcus Gaius and you are—?'

'Jodocca!' she returned.

He knew the British never had last names. 'Which tribe?'

A stab of caution had touched her mind and she prevaricated. 'From around,' she told him, moving one arm in a half circle, which could have meant anywhere. 'And you?' she wanted to know. 'Where are you stationed?'

A grin touched his lips, and he too waved one arm nonchalantly. 'Here and there. At the moment, let's say I have a roving commission.'

She was at a loss at what to do next, which he sensed. He took her arm and guided her away from the thick of the people so they could walk quietly, flashing probing looks at each other.

As they reached the outskirts of Colchester's fortification, he took her aside but kept hold of one arm. Tipping his head slightly, he studied her face, examining each feature, then, his eyes warm and friendly, he

5

looked deep into hers.

'Well,' was all he finally managed to get out and she had a flash of insight. He was affected as much as her. It was uncannily weird, because between them something pulled. She remembered one of the rare, confiding talks with her mother years before. Macha had admitted that once she had clapped eyes on Oslan, no other warrior had a chance for her hand and she had never, for one day, regretted her choice.

'What is it?' she whispered to him.

He had a deep voice, and now it was throaty. 'We call it a thunderbolt,' he replied. 'It's something rare but when it does happen between two people they are fortunate, smiled upon by all the gods.' He had paused and looked around, but they were discreetly alone. 'I was married but she died in childbirth. I am alone, but a serving officer and a true Roman.'

Jodocca shrugged. 'I am a widow also.' She eyed him with concerned eyes. 'I am a fighting warrior, and you Romans are the enemy of my people.'

'Rubbish! You wouldn't think that walking around here. I've seen Britons going out of their way to copy us and we welcome their cooperation.'

'Some!' she parried, sharply aware of an enormous cultural gulf as well as a political chasm.

'You are beautiful, quite magnificent,' he

6

had told her in a low voice, then wondered at the wry look on her face. 'I mean it!'

Jodocca had shaken her head, touched but unimpressed, though a little flattery was sweet. She thought him the most remarkable male she had ever met. Beneath his clothing she suspected there were huge, hard muscles, with no trace of fat. He was fine-featured, almost flashily good-looking, and conceited about his physical charms. If he was a widower what were the Roman matrons doing, leaving him uncaught? Was something wrong with him?

'I don't believe in beating women. Young boys and sodomy don't interest me. The reason I'm still footloose and fancy-free is from choice. Roman women come from one mould only, and one experience was more than enough,' he told her with a warm grin, reading her mind accurately. 'And you?'

Jodocca knew she had blushed. 'My first marriage was arranged, and what a wimp he turned out to be. Never again!' she explained firmly.

'You didn't love him?'

She shook her head. 'The next time I'll do the picking. Not my mother, and my father is now dead.'

'How long will you be here?' he wanted to know, suddenly anxious she might vanish overnight. He knew that this short and precious leave had only been granted pending a recall to active service. Where that would take him, he had no idea. They could not just part. He would not allow her to vanish into thin air. He had a shrewd idea as to where he would be stationed but his ingrained prudence stilled his tongue. He sensed it was the same with her.

Then it had been her turn to pause and reflect. She was loyal to her tribe, and he was, after all, the enemy. The fact they were on neutral ground meant nothing really but what if she never saw him again? She just could not let him vanish from her life. He was the most gorgeous specimen of manhood she had ever met, and her heart gave a sudden lurch at her predicament.

'A few days only,' she prevaricated slowly, 'then I have to return to my people.'

'Me too,' he told her soberly, then brightened. 'So that leaves us some time to get to know each other,' he offered hopefully. It occurred to him that though she did not name her tribe, there were ways and means of obtaining information. He knew there were always turncoat Britons more than willing to sell information for the appropriate number of silver denarii.

*   *   *

'So you spent just about a week with him?' Macha prodded uneasily.

Her daughter nodded, cheeks flushed, eyes perhaps just a little too bright.

Macha's heart sank. A thought entered her head, and she went stiff. 'Did you—?' she demanded.

Jodocca stiffened. 'No, I did not!' she started, knowing full well it was only because privacy had been hard to find without riding into the wild parts. 'And if I had, that wouldn't have been any of your business, Mother!'

'It would if you had been carrying a Roman bastard!' Macha snapped. 'So what happened in the end?' She was sharply curious to know, because around her daughter there was a strange new mantle. She had altered completely and her heart sank again. He would have to be a Roman! There were some magnificent British warriors so what curse had fallen on Jodocca to have a Roman mesmerise her? She quailed, foreseeing terrible future problems.

Jodocca shrugged unhappily. 'I arranged to meet him the next dawn to go riding, but he had left very abruptly. So then I left too!'

'By yourself, without any bodyguard! That was crazy!' Macha rebuked hotly. 'This nonsense stops right now; I'll see a new personal guard is appointed forthwith.'

Jodocca could not argue against this, but her lips went tight and thin. As a valuable British courier, as well as a fighting female of high tribal rank, she had to be protected.

There were no logical objections she could offer, and she felt her shoulders slump miserably. He had gone so suddenly, without even a message, and it was highly unlikely she would ever meet him again. All she could do was to carry his memory in her heart, and perhaps, one day in the future, she might hear news of Marcus Gaius.

Macha thought it prudent to change the subject. It almost broke her heart to see the sudden misery in her daughter's eyes but, on the bright side, it might mean she was slowly coming to her senses. Out of sight, out of mind?

She decided this was the appropriate time to change the subject. 'Lud is around,' she told Jodocca.

At once her daughter brightened. 'He is? That's wonderful! I will make a point of seeing him,' she said with fresh hope. Lud, a senior and very ancient Druid, who answered to no one, was like a favourite uncle to her and she loved him almost with ferocity. She could talk to Lud. He was so wise and understanding. Immediately she brightened, feeling her heart lighten with fresh hope.

'Where is he?'

Macha shrugged. 'Who knows?' she replied. Druids were the law, they answered to no one. They appeared and vanished, melting into the landscape and trees from paths and tracks few knew. There were three branches of this old, religious and legal organisation comprising bards, filidh and full Druids. Lud, the famous, was a full Druid.

Jodocca considered. There were many things she knew, which were unknown to her mother. She had a shrewd idea where Lud would hole out and await her, because the bond between them was extraordinarily close.

Macha's mind had moved on to more practical matters. Jodocca's news was something which she must consider closely later on. She was still horrified, but common sense had returned. Unless her daughter left the tuath and their tribal lands, it would be impossible for her to meet and develop a relationship with this upstart Roman. With luck, he might even be killed, especially if he was fool enough to venture in this direction.

'The Romans are still at the Fort with their odious Scapula as the commanding officer. Though the numbers aren't great yet, I have a suspicion more might be coming,' Macha said with disgust.

Jodocca pricked up her ears. 'That's interesting. I wonder exactly why Scapula is here?' she mused aloud. 'Prince Caratacus certainly opposes him, but he is much farther north. I expect we will end up with a glorious battle. When we win it, we can be left in peace,' she said hopefully, even though her common sense told her this had not yet been a Roman option.

11

'You'll be leaving, I suppose?' Macha asked wistfully. Jodocca was her sole, surviving offspring.

'Of course! I must report to Caratacus on the Roman strength at Colchester, and the general political situation. I expect I'll be gone all summer,' she warned her mother.

*   *   *

Macha surveyed her with a lump in her throat. Her daughter wore a bright red tunic of fine wool on which was pinned a brooch of gold shaped like a small stag. When she had travelled to Colchester she had been clad in a dull brown tunic and trousers but now she displayed her finery and rank. The latter was indicated by a torque of gold around her neck. Her trousers, called bracae, were of the same vivid scarlet, and her boots were a soft brown, made from fine, very supple leather.

They matched her waist belt from which hung the scabbard, which held her father's sword, whose blade she kept from rusting by wiping it regularly with mutton fat. On her hip was a viciously sharp dagger, which doubled as an eating tool. Her shield was round, constructed from hides and wood. It was decorated with red and green dyes, which had been splashed on almost haphazardly to make a gay pattern of stripes and blobs.

Macha nodded. 'Here are your

bodyguards,' she said, and Jodocca turned and flashed a smile. One held her horse, and she vaulted on its back, picked up the reins smoothly, and hefted her shield with the other hand. She threw a grin at Riothamus, the senior guard. He was twenty-seven, and a widower with no living child. He was highly intelligent, sharply suspicious and quiet. He never lost his temper, yet it was hard to make a friend of him. He was too serious for his own good at times, Jodocca told herself. Also, she knew he was a little too fond of her, which flattery only caused her quiet amusement.

To his rear was Ambiorix who, at thirty years old, was almost too old for the job, except he was a muscleman of incredible power. The trouble was that he had few brains but when his strength and bulk were required, Ambiorix was her man.

Bran rode to one side and beamed at her with pleasurable anticipation at whatever the day would bring. Bran was only a little older than his mistress, and he was filled with enthusiasm for life, but lacked general experience. Bran was a bit of a gamble as a bodyguard. He was happily married with one newly born son. His two previous children had died young, from the many diseases that abounded, especially those associated with birthing and which killed so many mothers too.

The last member was Bellovesus, who was a

13

shade older than Bran. No matter how long the gods allowed him to live, he would never lead. He had to be told exactly what to do, when and why. Working something out was beyond his capabilities, but he was loyal and brave to the death.

Jodocca threw a tiny nod to Riothamus who turned to Bran. 'Ride ahead and scout out that fort, but watch out for Roman patrols and those out foraging,' he warned.

'I shall eventually be heading for Prince Caratacus,' Jodocca told Riothamus, as they left the huts of her native tuath with Macha standing flat-footed and suddenly weary and miserable. 'But there is no great hurry, and I want to visit Lud first,' she explained.

Riothamus had already worked that out, and he eyed his mistress with some puzzlement. He had known her all his life, he respected and admired her, but now was baffled. Since her return from Colchester, she had altered. It was as if she had some enormous secret, and he wondered what it was. As her personal guard, sworn unto his death, he thought he knew everything about her and it niggled at him that she had some secret. He set his mind to work with remorseless logic.

As the track widened, the little group spread out. Jodocca rode alone as befitted her status, with Riothamus, directly at her horse's rear. With Bran gone, the others dropped to

14

the rear on both sides.

The sun had climbed, and it was warm for a spring day; Jodocca sniffed the air with pleasure as she allowed herself to dream the impossible, yet also felt pain in her heart. If they could have been left alone she knew she would have let Marcus have sex with her, which she knew he wanted. So did she. At times, when riding or walking with him, there had been that delicious wetness between her legs, accompanied by a pounding heart and she suspected he too had found himself in a difficult position more than once. She let her fancies twirl about—a life with such a man would be incredible. He had such strength and personality, yet her dreams never went farther. Always at this point, she remembered he was a member of the hated invading race, who had already taken so much of Britain. As if she could ever be a sedate Roman matron! It was ridiculous and stupid, yet how could she expect him to become a Briton? That was equally farcical, so with a deep sigh she succumbed to heartache and wished now that she had never gone to Colchester with a pack train of trade goods.

Jodocca's eyes roamed around. There was quite a large wolf pack in this immediate area, and in the cold months they were always on the lookout for whatever domestic stock they could steal. She kept a wary eye open for bear tracks. They were now out of their hibernation with cubs and at their most dangerous. It was always more prudent to ride around than confront the she-bear at this time of year.

As the track climbed upwards, so the landscape altered from forest to more sparse country with hard packed earth under the horses' hooves. At the peak Jodocca halted and looked around. On her extreme left was the antagonising Roman fort with its dreadful commanding officer, who at present, was also a governor of Britain. From this fort, the Romans had constructed a fine road, which ran direct to Gloucester where they had a very large garrison stationed. For a distance around this fort, there were always Roman patrols, and it was a dangerous area for the Britons.

'There's a horse coming, and fast too!' Jodocca said suddenly, and Riothamus stiffened and muttered a curse. The ears of his mistress had always been sharper than his, which niggled him. He tilted the head and now he too could hear hoof beats.

'That's Bran's mount,' he grunted, and hefted his spear. Jodocca moved her mount to the rear, and her men closed around her in a well-rehearsed drill from which she was totally protected against anything.

Bran thundered up, reining back so sharply his mount half-reared. 'My Lady!' he gasped. 'Romans coming!'

Jodocca was shocked. 'More Romans? How many?'

'On their road and hundreds of them. Listen!'

'Keep that damned horse still then!' Riothamus snapped, his temper shortening with worry. What was going on? Jodocca exchanged a look with him, the same question in her mind.

They could all hear the sound now even though it was still at a distance. It was a measured booming throb like that of distant drums. Jodocca felt a shiver chase down her spine, as she frowned at Riothamus. He knew what it meant and scowled. He loathed Romans.

'We must watch!' Jodocca said urgently.

Riothamus thought rapidly. 'One of those Roman miles ahead has a place where the land climbs a bit higher, and there are some trees in a little dip. We can leave the horses there and if we are lying flat away from the skyline, we won't be seen.'

'Let's go then!' Jodocca snapped, and dug her heels into her horse's flanks. They all broke into a gallop with Riothamus in the lead protectively. Jodocca's face was grim. She was perplexed by this information, and for a little while all thoughts of Marcus Gaius vanished. More Romans here had to mean something very serious.

They reached the dip, vaulted from their

17

horses and tied them to some scrubby bushes then ran after Riothamus. Near the top he held one hand out warningly, and they flopped to their bellies to inch forward.

Jodocca stared down with amazement and growing fear. The Roman marched on their road, in-line six abreast. Their accoutrements jingled. Their javelin gleamed, but it was their iron-shod boots that mesmerised. They marched in step, each boot hitting the ground at the same instant, and the drumming noise was explained.

The soldiers' necks and forearms were bare and weather-beaten. Each man wore a helmet, and all had an enormous shield, which hung over their back haversacks. Jodocca knew these were called scutums, and, when held in front, protected a Roman from chin to knee. She eyed the soldiers with a professional interest and guessed the scutums were made from thin sheets of wood, glued together with cross grain, then covered with red leather. Each was highly decorated, and they flashed in a pattern under the sun.

Every soldier had his personal pilum which was longer than a tall man, and all had vicious iron-hardened tips. Her attention turned to their dress. The upper part of the torso was covered with a leather jerkin, which comprised three iron plates. There were three more protecting the back, laced to the frontal ones. Still more plates were hooked from the waist and they swung as the men marched. Their pants were of leather, and she crinkled her nostrils.

A breeze arose from the Romans, carrying their odour, which was a combination of animal greases to prevent rust, oil which had been soaked into leather to keep it supple, and basic masculine sweat.

The boots continued to thud rhythmically, and it flashed through her mind that these hard boots were the power of Rome on the march. Her lips compressed.

Riothamus hissed a warning at her. 'They'll have scouts out, Lady.'

Jodocca knew this perfectly well but she was still too mesmerised to tear her eyes away. There was a sudden movement. A rider came thundering back from one side and rode up to the leader. This man was very different. His dress appeared the same but she noted bronze greaves on his legs. Some words were exchanged, then the first man pulled a whistle from his pocket. He trilled a peculiar note, but the soldiers continued to thunder past, though Jodocca could sense something was about to happen. The whistle chirruped a second time, and every boot slammed to an instant halt. A vast concourse of men acting as one. A third whistle sent them into action.

It appeared to be total confusion, but then Jodocca noted it was anything but. Instead, with their highly skilled and disciplined

19

organisation—tried and tested over the years—the Romans prepared to night camp. Men faced outwards towards where danger might appear, while others hurriedly, but purposefully moved around on specific tasks.

The man with the greaves, obviously, the commanding officer, stood apart and aloof, his broad shoulders towards them, and his helmet hiding his face until he half-turned. Jodocca caught her breath. It could not be! It was impossible, yet surely no two Romans had that particular stance. She frowned as her heart raced.

Riothamus fidgeted. 'My Lady!' he hissed urgently. 'We must leave.'

Jodocca slithered back and stood slowly, heart thundering. She flashed a look at Riothamus who fidgeted now to get his precious charge away from such a dangerous place. Foragers would appear at any time.

Jodocca untied her horse, mounted, then made up her mind. 'Just follow me and trust me, but do not be too close behind,' she ordered Riothamus firmly.

His nostrils pinched. Now what crazy idea had entered her head? There was no telling with this lady; and this situation he did not like one bit when they were only five fighters against hundreds below the skyline.

'We are all going to show ourselves,' Jodocca stated flatly, 'and I want to speak to that officer.'

Riothamus was appalled. 'Never!'

Jodocca forged into a canter, anxious to be alone for a moment with thoughts, which swirled in shocked delight and wary suspicion. She slowed to a walk, moving into the front as Bran took the point again. It was incredible to see Marcus once more, and not just as an ordinary soldier either. It had never entered her head that he might hold such high rank, and at this point, something else occurred to her. What exactly was he doing in their beloved Dubonnii territory?

Jodocca knew she had been far too careful to let slip the exact region of her tribe. So he could hardly be here to see her. So what was going on? She wondered if he had merely brought fresh troops to man the fort and would be taking others away with him. Yet surely such a high-ranking officer would not do so lowly a job, which could have been handled perfectly well by an ordinary centurion.

Riothamus studied her discreetly. Now what was eating her? It certainly concerned the Romans, yet their appearance could hardly be a surprise when Scapula had so few men at the fort. He turned this over in his mind because, deep down, he carried a torch for the lady. He had never tried to court her because his awe was so great, and until a few months ago she had been married. Although he now lacked her rank he considered himself

21

more than eligible to press a suit but he was unsure how to go about this. The lady was so self-assured and confident, part of him was inclined to hesitation, while the remainder of his self prodded him to act. The trouble was, she was so deep. Even her mother never really knew what she thought. He asked himself a little sourly where did that leave him? He was also highly conscious that he was savagely jealous of any male that went near her.

He flashed her another look. She was in a brown study, frowning slightly as if trying to solve a complicated mathematical equation, totally oblivious to the fact he rode half a length to her rear. Was it something to do with that Roman officer?

Jodocca was not as oblivious to her personal guard as he thought. She had long ago sensed, with sharp female instinct, that Riothamus's attentions towards her had changed in a subtle, positively irritating manner. Now that he had been promoted to be her personal guard she had a gut feeling it was going to irritate her. He was not her type of man at all. Her instinct also told her that, although he was loyal and incredibly brave, he had a sullen dangerous streak in his make-up. She muttered a curse, scowled and halted. She swung her horse around.

'I am going back,' she stated flatly. 'I want that officer to see me and talk to me!'

Riothamus was staggered, and temporarily

lost for words. He started to set his jaw in an obstinate line, but Jodocca forestalled him

'Don't even think of arguing with me, if you want to retain your position!' she snapped. 'I have my reasons so back we go and I will speak to that officer alone as well.'

'No!' Riothamus managed to get out at last.

'Yes! And if it comes down to it you will find I'm a better fighter than you, because I have more speed!' she said, knowing full well this clinched her position and argument, because no one doubted her word.

TWO

Senior Centurion Marcus Gaius, Primus Pilus, First Javelin of the XXth Legion was frustrated enough to make his temper sour and unpredictable. What made him even more furious was that he only had himself to blame, because he had not been as clever as he had thought.

His recall had been so abrupt there had been no time even to send a message. How could he hope to find one nondescript British female among the tribes of this wet island because find her he simply must. He would have no peace of mind until he did.

It was too stupid to the point of being ridiculous that a man in his position, of military seniority and with the mature age of twenty-five years should lose his heart to one wild, untamed, savage female—then he corrected himself. She might be wild—she probably was virtually untameable—but savage she was not. During that remarkable, glorious week, although she said little, what she did come out with were sentences of intelligence, indicating a sound education. He managed a wry grin of personal reproof. If she had been educated by those clever, but hated Druids, then she could well be higher up the intellectual scale than himself.

Dear Zeus! What had come over him? How could accidentally putting his well-shod foot upon hers have produced this internal madness? If anyone knew he would become the butt of the XXth, and, more to the practical point, not do himself much good either.

It was not that Rome objected to liaisons between her troops and native females; indeed, it was discreetly encouraged because the resultant sex kept soldiers even more amenable to Rome's harsh discipline. For officers though, especially of his status, it could prove another matter. He was privy to much that was top secret and, though he held no love for P Ostorius Scapula, the man did appear to have his wits about him. Certainly, the Senate approved.

He watched the troops while his mind

revolved in wild jerks. Every Roman soldier in the vast empire acted in the same way to a specific order. These booted footsloggers, the famous Caligates, were Rome's backbone. Every Roman fort and camp was laid out in the same, precise pattern, which was common sense. It decreed that a strange soldier in an unknown camp could find his way around in the pitch dark.

The sentries were in position and a foraging party ambled outside the camp's perimeter for fuel. Other men were busily erecting the usual ditch and bank on top of which would go a stout palisade. Each side would have a gate protected in turn by a detached length of pitch and bank which would run parallel to the main defence.

The latrines would stand just so, the fire would be there. Men would sleep on that spot, weapons would be neatly stacked in this position. Only wonderful Rome could invent such a system.

He moved a step and felt sweat trickle down through his greaves. He had set the men a cracking pace to burn up his anger, and could imagine the curses hurled behind his back. Tough! Do the men good! He sauntered into his tent, prepared for a strip-wash when he heard the century bellow a warning.

Instantly, he heard feet running and knew the camp was putting itself into an alert, defensive position. Now what, he asked himself, as he strode outside? There was still about an hour's daylight left. He felt the eyes of Centurion Lucius Crassus on him, which he ignored. The man was only just keeping his resentment bottled. He had hoped to command this relief detachment. Yet Marcus knew, quite a good man as he was, he lacked battle experience. It was a situation to watch though. A jealous brother officer could do untold harm if any snide remarks were allowed to drift in specific directions.

'Sir!' And Optio Crispus stood before him, at rigid attention. Marcus felt the first happy warmth entering his heart for a while. Now Crispus was his man without a doubt. He was a tough widower, hard as this island's climate, a ruthless NCO and highly intelligent. If anyone was officer material it was Crispus and Marcus had vowed to try and elevate him some day. He had been away from Rome for so many long campaigns that he moved and acted with the flavour of many countries and nationalities.

'What is it?'

'Natives have appeared. Just a small group of five. They are on the ridge of that hill, with one of their accursed female warriors in the lead.'

Marcus pushed Jodocca completely from his mind to concentrate upon this new, interesting situation. Was it a trap? He flashed a look around and saw his men were on full alert so this little group, even if they were a bait, would gain nothing.

He eyed their obvious leader. How crazy were these natives to allow such equal status to their women that they fought alongside their men, and they were, it was rumoured, twice as savage. He allowed himself to imagine a picture of a well-fleshed, beautifully dressed and perfumed Roman matron, then shot another look at the mounted female. She was heavily armed, and, from the way she held her weapons, obviously knew how to use them. She sat her mount with familiar ease yet he could guess how she would stink. What barbarians these people were not to bathe. A vision of Jodocca shot through his mind, and his forehead crinkled a second. It was true, he had arranged for her to experience the baths in the women's session, yet, even beforehand, she had not reeked like some of the Britons in the market town.

He caught a flash of yellow, and his eyes widened a little. 'She wears a golden torque,' he muttered, to his optic. 'Someone of rank, but what the devil does she think she's doing? Five of them against others.'

'I don't see how it can be a trap, sir,' Crispus said slowly, because the same thought had been his. 'Perhaps they are just testing us to see how alert we are—or just baiting us?'

Marcus took a deep breath. 'Possibly, but it seems to me she wants something. Oh very well. Never let it be said Rome did not respond to a female's gesture.'

'You are not riding after her, sir?' Crispus asked, shocked at the very idea.

Marcus turned to him. 'I can hardly indulge in a shouting match from here, can I?' he replied mildly. 'Get me a horse.'

'You are not going alone, sir. Myself and three others will come with you as escort. That makes the numbers even!'

Marcus did not deign to argue. Crispus was an excellent bodyguard, but, at times, inclined to overdo his mother-hen act. He looked up the slope again, then caught his breath. Surely not? He studied the female's saddle posture, then she moved a little, tilting her head slightly to one side in a mannerism that had become familiar over those seven days. It was her! He gasped, then struggled to keep an impassive look on his face as Crispus returned with selected men all suitably mounted and leading his best horse.

Marcos was staggered, delighted, but also perplexed. The girl to whom he considered he had lost his heart had appeared in the last place he expected and she was no mere native woman of little consequence. She appeared to hold higher rank and position than himself! He swallowed as he mounted, then trotted forward, mind reeling, heart thundering.

Four horse lengths' away, he turned and threw a hard look at Crispus who understood

28

but who showed his annoyance with tight lips, though he obeyed. However, a quick glance to right and left told the escort what to do. Weapons were loosened and held ready.

Jodocca missed nothing and she turned to Riothamus. 'You will all stay here. I will talk privately,' she ordered coolly. Damn all bodyguards, she thought, then, with a lump in her throat, she walked her horse forward. Shoulder to shoulder, the two mounts stood alone.

'You!' Marcus said in a low voice. 'I can hardly believe my eyes.'

Jodocca struggled to control her emotions. He must see how she felt, which would never do, here and now. 'My sentiment also,' she replied, huskily.

'By Jupiter!' and Marcus was just about at a loss for words, as his eyes swept over her. She sat there with such a regal bearing, an amazing contrast to the plainly dressed woman who had walked and ridden with him. Yet it was her! Those attractive features, that power of character, which swept front her like a tidal wave. Those discerning, vividly blue eyes—and he felt choked with what he wanted to say but dare not.

Jodocca drank in his magnificent stance in the saddle. Now fully dressed for fighting, he was even more splendid, and she caught her breath. The dual magnetism flowed between them again; each felt it, yet neither dared to speak with so many ears tuned to catch every word and nuance.

'We must meet!' he hissed urgently. 'Can you get away from those bodyguards of yours?'

Jodocca bit her lip. It would be difficult, but not impossible, if she used guile. 'What about you and yours?' she prevaricated.

Now, it was his turn to consider the virtually impossible. 'Perhaps,' he told her in a low voice.

'Dawn then,' Jodocca whispered. 'One of your Roman miles due east of here, through the trees. Follow the track at the top of the hill. There's an old oak, which was split by lightning, and I will be there tomorrow at dawn.'

'Done!' he snapped as he made up his mind. This was a god-given chance to try and arrange something, although how he would be able to slip away without Crispus breathing down his neck, he had no idea. Then another thought entered his head. Damn it all. He was the officer commanding these relief troops. What the hell was the good of such a position if he could not do what he liked now and again? He would fox Crispus by leaving early, and no century would dare to challenge him.

He leaned towards her again. His mind was working rapidly, while conscious of all eyes upon the pair of them. 'I'll say you have offered a temporary truce to explain this meeting,' he offered, tongue in cheek.

Jodocca saw through this instantly and smothered a smile, compounded of admiration for his genius and annoyance at such impertinence.

'This time—yes!' she agreed firmly.

He grinned wolfishly at her, his fingers itching to reach out and touch her, and he sensed that only something iron held her back. With feigned indifference, he lifted one arm in a Roman salute, wheeled his horse and turned back towards the camp. Crispus fell in alongside him, eyes narrowed with bewilderment, but too wise to question. One did not do that with any officer, let alone this one.

'A temporary truce, which will make our lives a little easier,' Marcus explained blandly. 'It will make a change for the men to go foraging without fighting at the same time.'

Crispus stifled a snort of exasperation. 'Pull the other one!' he told himself. Since when had guerrilla tactics bothered foraging Romans? What in Hades was his officer up to? He gave a tiny shake of his head, feeling deep unease in the pit of his stomach.

Lucius Crassus was also bewildered but his stolid features gave nothing away. It was true, temporary truces could often be arranged but here and now? And for what purpose? They were nearly at the fort so what was Gaius up to? Had he been given secret information in

London or elsewhere and, if so, from whom? The Senate? Caesar? Had that last short leave been nothing but put-up a job from start to finish? He writhed internally with jealousy. He hated the fact that secrets were kept from him, an officer and of a wealthy Roman family. In his opinion, he had been hard done by where promotion was concerned.

Riothamus squirmed. His lady had approached that Roman just a little too easily with an assurance that was uncalled for. It was as if she knew him, which was impossible for a loyal, true Dubonnii member. Or was it? He thought back. Why had the lady been so delayed in returning after a simple trading expedition? And riding back without an escort was foolhardy in these times. With pinched nostrils, almost squirming with jealousy, he took a deep breath, wondering whom he could consult, then decided to give more thought to the subject, because there was something here which stank.

Jodocca road back to her village, thinking rapidly as she worked out excuses for such a rapid return. Macha would be delighted, but their Tuath leader was a fat old fool, of no consequence in Jodocca's mind. The elders were rather trusting, where she was concerned, yet her reason had to be plausible, and she brightened as the solution hit her.

She was now going to see her distant cousin Caratacus and she had not seen Lud for a while. That was perfectly acceptable to everyone, though she could feel the hard glare from her chief bodyguard, his eyes boring into her shoulders. Was he going to become a nuisance, she asked herself soberly? If so, it would be better to get rid of him now but who else was there with his vast experience? It flashed through her mind that if Riothamus had started to feel jealousy whenever she eyed any male, he could even be dangerous. Then she shrugged; this was a problem she must shelve for the time being.

It was all easier than she had envisaged. She stayed the night in the guest hut, making a thin excuse to her mother who, though delighted to see her back, also gave her a penetrating stare, but mercifully refrained from questions.

Jodocca left a docile mare on the fringe of her village and, hardly sleeping from pent-up excitement, moved silently through the night after just a brief explanatory word with a somewhat sleepy sentry. The roaming hounds sniffed her curiously, surprised at her early appearance but, apart from a few questioning whines, they did not bark. She slipped away like a wraith, riding at a sober walk until clear of her people. With expert knowledge of the area, she then increased the pace, heart thundering with delicious expectation.

She slowed to a walk as the damaged tree appeared, outlined starkly against a sky that already showed a few pink tinges in the east. She studied the area, weapons at the ready, then spotted his horse. He stepped forward, from where he had been leaning against a tree trunk and held her horse as she slid down. Carefully he fastened both animals together, then turned, warmth filling his eyes.

'We did it!' he gloated and opened his arms wide.

Without thought or hesitation Jodocca flung herself against him. She felt powerful muscles encase her in a bear hug and marvelled at his power, then her head was tipped back, and his lips fastened on hers with hunger. She felt almost overpowered by his virility and, even through his defensive leather, she felt a huge rock-hard penis, and instantly she flooded between her legs.

Finally, gasping for breath, she eased herself away, and stood with her head on his chest listening to the drumming of his heart while he stroked her hair. She closed her eyes, savouring his scent, wondering at the trembles in her thighs, then he gave a sigh, pushed her back and, leaning against a tree, studied her.

'Do you realise you have turned my life upside down?' he asked her, but paused for another kiss before he continued: 'I'm head over heels in love with you, you fighting Briton!'

Jodocca felt ridiculous tears fill her eyes. When had she last wept? She felt her shoulders sag, marvelling at this rawness of being enfolded and protected. It was strange, unknown, but not at all unpleasant.

He let his hands explore her figure. The Britons never wore body armour, so his hands had free play over full, ripe breasts, a slender waist and lovely round buttocks.

'I could take you here and now,' he hissed in her ear, his voice hopeful.

Jodocca chuckled. She knew she would respond if he did. This man's mesmeric power left her defenceless.

'And I wish I could stay long enough,' she told him sadly. 'It's difficult being guarded all the time,' she ended ruefully.

He nodded. 'I have the same problem. When I do ride back, my senior NCO will no doubt play hell with me as far as rank allows. What are we going to do?' he asked wistfully. 'I want you as my wife. Will you marry me?'

Jodocca hesitated now as her heart and head battled. 'There is nothing I'd like more,' she admitted, 'but we are on opposite sides,' she reminded him. 'What chance is there for us?'

'Other Britons have married or cohabited with Romans,' he said quickly, anxious to breach her defences further.

Jodocca had to be honest. 'I could never be a Roman matron,' she told him flatly. 'I'm used to being free, doing as I like, and this is my land, my people.'

'Oh Jodocca!' he groaned. 'Why don't you tribes realise Rome is here to stay, and what harm do we do? We have brought nothing but good with us for those tribes who co-operate. We have brought roads, sanitation, paths, central heating, education—'

'Oh no!' she interrupted. 'Not the last. Our Druids are the wisest, cleverest men in the world. Their knowledge goes back to before Rome existed. Those educated by the Druids consider themselves very fortunate. And I was one,' she said, finishing in fluent Latin.

He was startled, and suddenly uneasy. 'There is an edict against all the Druids,' he told her. 'I myself have no time for them because they agitate the tribes—'

'Why not?' she challenged, a bite in her voice. 'This is our land. It is our country. We were all quite happy until you invaded. You'll never conquer all of us, and I predict there will be uprisings and one day the Romans will be driven from our shores!'

They drew apart, though still held hands. 'Don't we have a chance then? Me and you? Is that what you are saying?' he asked sadly.

Jodocca sighed heavily. 'Would you turn traitor to Rome?' she asked him gently. 'You asked me to do that to my people!'

'No I don't!' He hastened to explain. 'We could go somewhere else. An officer like me finds it easier to leave military service than do rankers. Anyhow, I've done my share for

Rome. I could become a civilian here in Britain. I'm not exactly poor. We could go—' and his mind hunted frantically, '—south—anywhere, you pick. I'll build us a superb villa, lay in the best hyper cast for hot water that you have ever seen. We could get to explore each other's culture, then we could engage in the arts. And I would pick somewhere with a theatre or an arena. If you wanted we could travel but our home will be here. Surely you too can resign your position?'

Jodocca knew she could. Perhaps even more easily than him, but how could she then live with a conscience? Had he thought of that? Sadly, she shook her head, her womanly instincts more practical than his.

'It would not work,' she told him sorrowfully. 'I think we'd both end up looking over our shoulders, remembering, and both regretting. Perhaps one day life will change,' she ended hopefully, like a child wanting a gift.

He knew that this was more than possible. It was downright likely and not as she envisaged. 'Come with me!' he urged. 'Leave your people. Make your own life with me!'

Jodocca hesitated again, torn painfully. She could leave, she knew that but she felt he was stampeding her and she had promised, on her precious oath, to report direct to Caratacus. 'Ask me again before winter sets in,' she prevaricated. 'Come to my village by which time I will have had ample time to think things through. You should do the same as well,' she ended wisely.

He saw that it was almost full daylight. He must leave soon, or there would be hell to pay because of his absence, which could easily play into the itching hands of Lucius Crassus. He wondered if he was going to be sent back to Gloucester with the relief troops; then let Crassus find out what real command was like under bad-tempered Scapula!

'All right,' he agreed reluctantly. 'At your home,' he confirmed, not adding that, by then, most of Britain, and certainly her own tribal land, would be under Roman rule. He felt sick at this—how would she react? Would love turn to hatred?

Jodocca felt a little uplift to her heart. If all went well—and why shouldn't it?—Caratacus would have planned properly, and the Romans would be beaten, and it would simply be a case of driving them back over the sea. When she had done her duty to her cousin she would be morally free to plan and live her own life. Her heart filled with sudden warmth, as she smiled up at him.

'Now we had better go and put our respective bodyguards out of their misery,' he grinned, almost like a little boy, 'though I expect we are both going to be verbally disciplined for it. Rank may have privileges, but it also creates problems.'

'I agree with that!' she said and, standing on tiptoes, kissed him with lips filled with hopeful promise.

THREE

Platon lowered his head and muttered to himself in anger. He knew he was very near the pitch of revolt, yet something stilled his hand. Certainly, he had had more than enough of being in a legion, any legion at any time. During the past few weeks he had found himself in constant trouble through what Optio Crispus described as dumb insubordination. Of course, that arrogant showman swine Optio Marius would have to concur. Thank Jupiter that, at least, he was a full legionnaire and not an auxiliary like Marius who, as German-born, did not qualify. Platon was Rome-born but a soldier's life had palled.

It was true, no one awaited Platon's return to Rome, and life in the legion was secure but as a low ranker, with no foreseeable promotion, his money was limited to 150 denarii a year.

Like many other men of his grade he came from a poor family and the secure profession of a soldier had appeared to offer a fine life. Upon retirement, there was the good bait of an award of land or cash. Marius would also be able to claim Roman citizenship, even though an auxiliary, provided he stayed the course.

In exchange, though, a man had to sign away twenty-five years of his life, because only officers qualified for short-term engagements. Quite suddenly, Platon's heart squeezed with misery as he looked down endless years with optios like Crispus and Marius forever breathing down his neck. Yet, what could he do? It was a problem that had commenced as a tiny niggle, but during the past week had grown to a mighty tree of resentment.

Now the latest gossip was that they might be relieved temporarily, which would mean another forced march back to Gloucester and, if they were lucky, a few days to sample the fleshpots and then be posted where?

The trouble was that Marius had taken a dislike to him, and Crispus did nothing to intervene. The German was a big man, coarse, crude, and with a vicious streak of natural cruelty in his makeup. Platon had no redress because to turn on someone of higher rank would be fatal. It was simply because Marius was jealous of a man below him in rank but who had natural Roman citizenship because of his birthplace.

Platon polished the metal parts of his shield and threw a look around at the companions of his maniple. They were content, almost happy, and certainly spoiling for a fight with the British. Rudis, Eldon and Platon had been together from the start of their training but Platon was aware he had grown apart from them. Rudis was a joker with shallow thinking while Eldon was more than happy to have every hour organised for him by the optios, with no wit to look into the future.

This morning he was supposed to be paid but Platon had calculated there would be little due to him. It was not worth joining the queue, with all the fines the Optio had exacted, to say nothing of constant latrine duties. Those men who valued their money would deposit it, while the feckless ones would get involved in gambling games.

What also stuck in his throat was the fact all soldiers had to buy their own food from the commissary supplied by Rome. He had worked out that this took a third of a man's pay and though this still left a good sum it was not enough when fines had to be paid and equipment replenished if lost or damaged.

Those without enough money for food would be forced to take out loans and pay interest. It was all right for the cavalry who received 200 denarii a year while the really crack troops earned 300.

He forced his mind back to practicalities and knew he had to make a final decision, because he was sick of Rome, and this life. If he failed in an attempt to run away and was caught he would have to suffer a very unpleasant death, but suddenly he did not care. Platon gave a grunt and slipped a pair of lightweight, smooth-soled British shoes under his tunic. Roman boots were solid and substantial, but very easy to track and he blessed the foresight that had prodded him to buy these shoes at Gloucester from a hard-up Briton. Wearing them, he would be difficult if not impossible to track and he knew he was ready. To bolt, to run and desert was Rome's most heinous crime, but he was desperate to try and make a fresh life or die in the process. Rome could go to hell.

Crispus appeared from nowhere and Platon started. 'You, you and you!' he barked and pointed. 'Get out there, forage for wood for the fires. Well, come on then! Jump to it!'

Platon realised he would never have a better opportunity, and he sprang into action. With the others he raced around and grabbed his weapons, and a small phalanx of them trotted away from the camp, with two others on their flanks as guards.

Platon's heart hammered as Eldon waved with his hand for them to spread out to gather dead timber but they would still have to keep within close distance of their flank guards. He saw Rudi was nearest, and when he saw a likely clump of bushes he nodded towards it. 'Have to crap!' he said bluntly, and Rudi threw him a nod of understanding.

Platon trotted forward, and behind the bushes he acted fast. He hastily pulled off the heavy marching boots and slipped the lightweight British shoes on his feet. Then he took a deep breath and with his shorter pilum, in his hand, dagger on one side of his belt and javelin attached to the other, he looked around swiftly.

Right away, he spotted an animal track, stepped silently onto it, threw one more quick glance to his rear and bolted in a steady lope. It was a mile-consuming gait which he knew he could keep up for hours. As he ran he calculated. He headed east by north, which would do for the time being to get him away from the fort's jurisdiction.

Soon he was sweating, but he breathed easily and as one trail ended he stepped onto another, which headed in his selected direction. He had no food with him, which was a bad debit point but he could hunt for small game and eat the meat raw. Lighting a fire would be very foolish. If the Romans did not find him the British would and meeting them just yet was not desirable. He had to pick the time and place and just hope that his prowess as a trained soldier would appeal to them. His gamble was that once he had proved himself they would adopt him as a Briton. If they did not, they might just as well kill him.

By dusk, he guessed he was many Roman miles away and slowed to a walk. His hardened legs were not tired, but his belly was empty. There was no game around, it had vanished for the night and he wondered where he might hole up. Sleep was vital. A cave would be handy, but one seemed unlikely in this terrain. He strolled into a small clearing and, overhead, he could just make out a new moon, where the leaves did not quite meet. Somewhere to one side, a stream tinkled and on the left he saw the ground was more elevated.

Abruptly, he braked. His senses screamed a warning and instantly he went on to battle alert as the skin at the nape of his neck crinkled. His sharp eyes spotted the other first, and he lifted a weapon in readiness but slowly lowered it.

The ancient was taken by total surprise, and he stood stiffly, knees bent with age. He had a spear, a tiny flimsy thing, which a child would have used and bravely he hefted it in warning.

Platon was amused and lowered his weapon completely. He had only a few words of one British tribal tongue, so he used the universal gesture of placing his weapons aside and opening both hands, palms forward in peace.

The ancient gave a low call, and to Platon's surprise another equally old man appeared and this time he caught his breath. The newcomer was incredibly old with a wizened face, bowed shoulders and stringy thin hair above a face criss-crossed with many age lines.

He wore a dirty robe and Platon knew instantly he was a Druid. The other would be his guard and servant. Some guard, Platon mused to himself. A child of five could do better.

He gave a shake of his head and regarded the Druid thoughtfully. A pair of deep grey eyes returned the compliment when suddenly, almost without knowing what he was doing, Platon, ducked his head in a polite bow of respect to age, wisdom and seniority.

The Druid smiled gently, warmth flooding his eyes as he studied the dishevelled Roman and instantly knew his story. He gave the tiniest shake of his head. This man was either brave, a fool or desperate. He knew only too well the harshness and the incredible cruelty of Roman discipline. However, he was not wanted here, which was a holy spot. The Druid lifted his right hand and pointed ahead at an angle.

Platon understood. He threw a small smile of thanks and broke into a trot once more, running easily in the very last traces of evening light. Within seconds he had vanished, and shortly afterwards, the sound of his passage had gone too.

'Well!' Osa said. 'He gave inc a shock, appearing like that!'

Lud grinned. 'You are nearly as old as me. So what do you expect?'

Osa growled something under his breath,

and Lud chuckled. Osa was having one of his irritable days, which meant he was suffering from the joint ills in his knees. He always became tetchy on such days, but what could they expect at their ages?

'I'm going back inside,' Lud said, knowing perfectly well that Osa in a bad temper would ignore this. 'I am expecting another visitor, and'—he paused, tipped his head to one side, with one hand behind an ear—'there's a noise coming towards us, and that will be . . . ' His voice died away with pleasurable expectation.

When Jodocca and Riothamus rode into the tiny clearing only Osa was visible, rubbing one of his knees, his toy spear lying carelessly on the earth.

Riothamus shook his head. These two were not fit to be let loose anywhere and, to be wandering among the tribes alone, they were mad. They should have at least a guard of two fine young men, but he knew better than to suggest anything. Besides, he could not be bothered. His mind was fully occupied with his own thoughts and problems, which he knew would require considerable cogitation before action.

Jodocca grasped Osa's hands and beamed at him, noting the pain lines in his face, and understanding. She bent forward and pecked a kiss on one gnarled cheek. Thence she was both amazed and amused to see the old man flush, grunt and jerk his head aside.

She grinned to herself. Who would have thought it possible to embarrass Osa? She walked up the path to where a tiny hut was partially concealed and halted outside.

'Lud?' she called in a low voice. It was better not to go in unannounced because Lud was still perfectly capable of driving a knife between an intruder's ribs.

'Come!'

She stepped past a crude hanging curtain, which deflected the glow of a little fire. The Druid sat on a stool, toasting his toes by the fire; he smiled as she approached, sank down gracefully and bowed her head with respect.

'It took you long enough to come!' Lud grumbled at her. 'What have you been up to?'

Jodocca took a deep breath, then related the events of the past few weeks, though she suspected very little might be new, because Lud's system of acquiring information was one developed through all the tribes—it would have staggered and horrified the Romans if they had known. News at the far end of the land could swiftly reach a northern tribe, passing from mouth to mouth, vouched as coming from a very respected Druid.

He listened to her in silence and studied her carefully, then, when she had finished, he eyed her thoughtfully. Under his sharp scrutiny Jodocca knew she had turned scarlet, and she broke eye contact first.

'Why haven't you told me all?' Lud asked

47

gently. 'Am I no longer worthy of your confidence?' he chided.

Jodocca met his gaze, then shook her head. 'I'm in awful trouble, Lud.'

'I know,' he said simply. 'It shows in your mannerisms. I think you are in love with a man your mother and the others would consider totally unsuitable!'

Jodocca no longer hesitated. 'I am. He is and he's a Roman—an officer and he wants me to leave my people!'

'Can you?' he asked seriously. She was his great favourite for reasons that she did not know. It crossed his mind that this might be an appropriate time to do his share of the talking. He suspected he did not have much longer to go.

Jodocca, thought, then answered honestly. 'Not yet,' she admitted. 'First I have my sworn duty to report to Caratacus, and to fight by his side. After that, if I live—who knows?'

Lud considered. 'What does he offer you in exchange for giving up your tribe?'

She told him all, omitting neither word nor gesture. He thought it an excellent offer, bearing in mind the knowledge he held and the future which he sensed.

'What shall I do, Lud?'

He shook his head. He could have told her, but refused. There were times when a person had to follow his own destiny alone. No matter what the decisions were they could not

48

be shared. Advice was not always wise. 'You decide that alone,' he told her flatly, 'but, whatever you do decide, think wisely. Do not do something you will regret in later life when you are old, alone and crippled with aches and pains. When age comes, it is nice to share it with another,' he replied meaningfully.

Jodocca pricked up her ears. Now what was that supposed to mean? The trouble with Lud, like all true Druids, was his inclination to answer in riddles. A meaning had to be hunted for and often there were two possible interpretations, each in an opposing direction.

'I will tell you that life is changing,' Lud told her heavily. 'Whether it is for better or worse is questionable. I will tell you something, though,' and he pointed. His right foot moved in some dust and outlined a crude fish. 'If anyone crosses your path, setting great store upon this sign, pay attention.'

'A fish?' she murmured, completely mystified.

'It is a new religion,' Lud explained, 'because Druidism is dying out.'

'No!'

Lud shrugged. 'Nothing lasts forever. Life moves on, it's progress. This is but the natural order of things. I doubt you'll ever see me again.'

She was deeply shocked, and tears instantly prickled in her eyes. She opened her mouth to speak, but no words came.

'You think about what I've said,' Lud insisted. 'Many years ago, when I was young and lusty, I fancied a girl. Oh! She was a rare beauty but I was already committed to the Druids. And I chose them instead of her, though I had some lovely and lively times with her before I vanished for training.' He paused, thinking back down a long line of years, while she sat opposite, mesmerised by this new story.

'What happened?' she whispered, enchanted at seeing a new side to this ancient whom she loved dearly.

'She had a baby. My baby. She had married another, but I knew the child was mine, and, ever since, I have kept a discreet eye on the females of that family.'

'You should have married her instead,' Jodocca rebuked softly.

Lud chuckled to himself. 'Any idea who that baby girl was?'

Jodocca frowned. 'How on earth could I?'

Lud laughed at her then, finally amused. 'They called her Macha!'

Jodocca stared at him, totally speechless with shock as she understood at last. 'My mother!' she gasped. 'So you are my grandfather!' she cried with delight. 'That explains why I've always felt such empathy and love for you!'

She jumped up and flung herself against him, revelling as his thin arms clasped her, and she leant back and gently stroked his withered cheek. Her heart was swollen with joy as tears flowed freely. 'I wish I had known before!'

'It was never easy to tell you. Nor the other way, for you to learn from your mother. Anyhow, I swore her to silence years ago!'

'Oh, Grandfather, all those wasted years!' she groaned, then a thought struck her. 'Are you telling me to go with the Roman?'

He shook his head, sadness showing in his bleary eyes where cataracts could be seen. 'Before you can make any decision about this Roman, I have to tell you that you will experience sadness, grief and terrible danger. If you survive all these in one piece then will come the time to make the decision concerning the rest of your life. Remember, child, you are well bred. Your father was a mighty warrior. You have it in you to rise above that which would decimate others. And only you, in the end, can make the choice—no one else, and that includes me!'

'I don't understand you,' she told him miserably. It would be very dark outside now, and high time to return to the vill and then it would be her duty to ride off north. She took a deep breath and flashed a wan smile. She would think about it all later. Much later. 'And you?'

'We leave with the dawn, we will head to the next holy grove. There are other tribes to visit. I must spread news of the Romans while I am able.'

'You should have an escort!' she protested. 'There are so many more Romans at the fort.'

Lud snorted. 'Don't teach me to suck eggs, Granddaughter. I was dodging enemies before you were born,' he snapped with some asperity. 'Only us tribal people know all the holy groves. The Romans have no idea! Now get yourself off, get back to your vill; your mother will be deeply concerned—and try to stop arguing with her so much. When all is said and done, my daughter means well!' and he grinned mischievously at her.

Jodocca knew a dismissal when she heard one and she stood reluctantly. Riothamus would be like a bear with a sore head, riding through the dark. Again it flashed through her mind she should replace him, then she pushed that thought to one side. There was not really time to chop and change personal bodyguards now. She hugged the old man once more and was thoughtful as she rode back to her vill.

The next morning she told her mother everything, her voice low and sad while Macha listened thoughtfully. 'I wish I had known before,' she said slowly.

Her mother understood and nodded sagely as well as sadly. 'I too wished you had known, but there was nothing I could do. I was sworn to secrecy by Lud. So when do you leave for the north?'

'In another twenty-four hours. We shall pass the holy glade so I shall make a short detour just to make sure Grandfather got on his way safely,' she explained to her mother who nodded with approval.

'I think you had better take Verica with you. She's been lost since her man Heg died from the belly illness, and Kei is all she has left now of that marriage. She has to get another husband, and it will be better if the tribe has some fresh blood. Kei is thirteen and adult. Take them both with you,' she suggested.

Jodocca was not sure of this and hesitated. Macha did not. 'You have a duty there. When your father was alive and the chief he always looked after the widows and Verica is an excellent chariot driver though a rotten horsewoman. Kei would make a first-class scout too. That boy has nothing to learn about the wild.'

Jodocca groaned. 'I don't care for Verica. She's such a wishy-washy person,' she grumbled.

Macha had no mercy. 'All the more reason for you to develop her then,' she snapped. 'Don't tell me two more pairs of eyes won't be useful when moving through strange territory. Remember, you have to get through Gloucester and the Romans are very strong there. If you make a slightly larger group, you can easily pass yourself off as horse traders,' she suggested cunningly.

Jodocca eyed her mother with narrowed eyes. 'What is behind all this?' She paused. 'Come on, Mother. You do nothing without a reason,' she challenged.

Macha tossed her head. 'Well, if you must know that potbellied old fool, Vercingetorix, has become too idle to run the tuath and the elders have kicked him out. He went yesterday. All in a huff, and hurt pride, the waddling all fool!'

'Where has he gone?'

Macha let out a snort. 'To join the vicus at Gloucester, so be very careful when you go through there. I don't trust him at all. He will do anything for Roman denarii, but they are not fools either. They will soon see through him and treat him accordingly. Be sure, though, he will tittle-tattle to try and curry favour with the Romans so from now on treat Gloucester as a very dangerous place. And this is why you need extra eyes.'

Jodocca nodded thoughtfully. Macha was quite correct. Extra eyes, and especially young ones, would be invaluable, and, after all, she did not really have to associate with Verica. She could always hold herself aloof, by virtue of rank and general position. 'Very well,' she agreed. 'We will all leave in the morning, ride gently, check that Grandfather got away all right, circumnavigate Gloucester, if necessary, and then up to Caratacus.'

FOUR

Marcus was torn. His report to Scapula had been satisfactory, though what exactly had been in the sealed document he had passed over had not been immediately apparent. What had shocked him, though, was Scapula's condition and temper. The man seemed ill, almost on the point of a physical breakdown, which boded bad for Rome. Who else was there on this island to take the governor's place if Scapula died suddenly? Then he had dismissed this thought. It was not his problem.

He had been given his orders: a rather surprising second, roving commission to take relief men back to Gloucester, and then to head north with an escort. Obviously, the war was going to be taken into the homeland of Caratacus. Naturally, he would take Crispus with him. When quite alone they had a good degree of camaraderie, which was strictly forbidden for the sake of discipline when others were around. He did pause to wonder, though, just how much it would be prudent to confide in Crispus. What would be his reaction if he knew his senior officer was wildly in love with a Briton?

His thoughts returned to Jodocca. He wanted to see her again quite desperately, especially now he was going to be away from this area for what could be a long period. Where was she now? What was she doing? Was she thinking of him? He gritted his teeth with frustration, then made his mind switch to practicalities.

He would march the relief men back to Gloucester, but the pace would have to be slow. There were some men in this contingent who would have to be retired through injury so instead of doing a very rapid forced march they would need to camp en route.

Yesterday, he had ridden out with the forage party for exercise, though mostly in the wild hope he might see her again. In that he had been disappointed, so he had made another practical decision. Before he left he would visit her vill and explore. It would be a legitimate exercise to weigh up the fighting men available in this region, the condition of their horses, the state of any weapons that they may have, and generally poke and prod into their affairs. He would be hated, of course, and that worried him not one iota just as long as he could see her again.

Crispus marched up, eyebrows elevated in a silent question. He felt uncomfortable because there was something going on with his officer, which he could not understand.

'I intend to visit that nearby British settlement and have a general snoop around,' Marcus told him. 'An edict went out a little while ago that Britons can only have weapons for hunting. War weapons are banned though I expect they've been hidden somewhere handy.'

Crispus looked him straight in the eyes and wondered yet again. That sounded like the best excuse he had heard for a long time, because such senior officers did not waste their time with those matters that could be dealt with quite adequately by lower ranks. He made a firm decision that when they were finally alone and heading northwards he was going to ask some pointed questions, even if they did produce a tongue lashing.

Marcus read his mind. The ride north was going to be lively and interesting. 'Come on! Let's go and stir up that British vill—we might even find a hornet's nest!' He grinned wolfishly.

Crispus bellowed a few terse orders, while a dozen men collected horses and weapons. Marcus's attention was attracted by a soldier, who stood nearby at rigid attention as one with nothing specific to do. He saw wistfulness in the man's eyes.

'Who are you?' he snapped.

The soldier was shocked. Since when had an officer last spoken to him? He could not remember because he was too insignificant. 'Signifier Sellus, sir!' he replied quickly, and waited with apprehension.

Marcus ran his eyes over him. He was in his

57

late thirties, quite a nondescript, just another ranking soldier, and he held himself very stiffly as if favouring one side.

'What's wrong with you?' Marcus wanted to know.

'Shoulder wound, sir! It never healed properly, so I've put in for an honourable discharge.'

'Are you Roman?'

'I am, sir!' Sellus replied proudly—not that it had ever done any good. He was just another lonely man from a very poor family, who had jumped at the chance to have a secure life as a soldier.

'Going back to Rome, then?' Marcus asked quietly.

Sellus shook his head firmly. 'Nothing to go back for, sir,' he explained. 'Anyhow, I've been here so long. I like this island, even the weather!' he dared to joke.

'Do you have a woman?' Marcus was interested, and he knew such a conversation was excellent for boosting morale. Too many officers made the mistake of ignoring the rankers; simply using them as javelin fodder while such men had always interested him.

'Not one I'd shack up with permanently, sir!'

Marcus grinned at him. 'Then you can come with me now, and cast your eyes upon the local talent,' he offered, eyes twinkling. 'You might find someone worth pursuing if you don't mind her being British!'

'Yes, sir!' Sellus cried, and beamed his delight.

Marcus felt the eyes of Crispus upon him and his optio nodded approvingly. Apart from his genuine feeling for the rankers, Marcus knew there was more to it than met the eye. Rome thoroughly approved of retiring soldiers settling in foreign lands. These men always made an excellent reserve and should trouble lift its ugly head what better men were available than those who had been trained by Rome? He would get a decent land grant and a pay-off fee quite enough to spend the remainder of his days in Britain.

Sellus appeared in seconds, mounted, armed and grinning from ear to ear. This was quite splendid! A chance to get far away from the fort for a while, and his fellow soldiers. In his spare time he had devoted himself to playing Twelve Lines or War Game Soldiers at which he was something of an expert. He had his own board, with the necessary eight rows of eight squares and a splendid set of fifteen pieces, which he had painstakingly carved himself. A man could not play this game all the time though and he was wise enough to realise that when discharged he might be very lonely indeed. Besides, it would be nice to have regular sex without paying over the odds for it with whores—when you could even get near them.

For months he had had a dream. He had always been thrifty with his money, rarely gambling it away and anticipating the grant and the land which would be his, he had had the temerity to draw up plans for a little villa. It would not be large, but it would have a heated floor, so there would be plenty of hot water for baths. But without a female companion . . . ?

He had attended a slave market when in Gloucester and eyed the women on offer, but they were either too subdued, too sullen or too treacherous. And Sellus did not want a slave when it came to the crunch. He wanted a proper wife and this officer's offer was most providential.

He knew a lot more than many other men about the area because he had always paid attention, listened to all the gossip without joining in and picked up some words of the local tribal tongue. He knew all about the locals as well. He also knew a useless chief had been thrown out to live at Gloucester in the vicus which fringed the Roman fort. He also knew a tough woman named Jodocca had her home there and she had a widowed mother, someone of his own age group.

Although Sellus knew he was no oil painting, he was as tall as the next man, well muscled with a rough, weather-beaten and rather craggy face. He still had thick dark hair, long flattened from constant helmet wearing and he considered he had worn rather well. Could he be lucky enough to find a woman who agreed? The most likely candidate appeared to be the new chief, the woman called Macha, so with palpitations of hope he followed his officer as they rode off.

It was good land, Sellus noted. A man could do a lot worse than settle in this region as long this Dubonnii tribe were pacified and he knew that would be soon. Who could stand up to Rome's power? With pleasurable expectation, he entered the vill, dismounted and plodded around, following orders in looking for forbidden war weapons

Marcus sat his horse as befitted his rank and studied the area. What a poverty-stricken hole was his first thought. After affluent Roman villas, these rudely constructed huts were quite pathetic. How was it that people who lived like savages could be such awesome foes? No wonder they stank when he met them at markets, because there was not a bath house in sight.

Yet this was her home! From here she had sprung, and he looked at the sullen Britons with renewed vigour. They were angry at the Romans' arrival, and, though they dared not do anything against such heavily armoured troops, they showed their fury with a sullenness that was dangerous.

He carefully looked around as his men entered the huts searching for weapons, which could be used in time of war. They would not find any, of course. These Britons were far too fly to have anything but hunting weapons here. Somewhere, though, they would have a cache and Marcus knew it would be so hidden it would be beyond their ability to find them. This venture was nothing more than a gesture to remind these people to keep their place. Don't lie to yourself, he argued honestly, you have come snooping, hoping to find her here. Although his men bustled about, doing perhaps just a little more pushing and shoving than was strictly necessary, they did not appear to protest.

There were some young men here, though, Marcus observed. There were quite a few children, and how healthy and fit they looked, despite these barbaric living conditions, but they were not many. Disease was obviously a killer, which was no great surprise, considering all this filth. Even their latrine area was not properly attended to; he could smell it from where he sat.

Their domestic cattle were few in number, which meant they slaughtered in the autumn, because they had no way to preserve carcasses. Hadn't they heard of smoke and salt? The remaining breeding stock were of reasonable quality, which point caught his eye.

The small group of elders huddled to one side. They showed no fear, and their outrage was contained. At any moment he knew someone would come storming over to protest at his intrusion. Then he heard a short screech and a very loud smack. Suddenly one of his men came hurtling backwards from a hut followed by a furious female. He jumped forward and, before his men could do anything, she let fly again with a powerful right hand. It caught the trooper flash on his right cheek with sufficient power to bowl him on his backside.

Marcus smothered a grin as the soldier stumbled to his feet, red-faced with embarrassment and humiliation, caught his officer's eye and backed away to stumble elsewhere.

Marcus turned his attention to the woman and was stunned with shock. She glowered up at him, her eyes blazing with rage, fair hair whipping with temper, her large, very ample breasts shaking as she prepared to frame words to hurl up at him.

He gasped, his jaw dropping with shock. This was how Jodocca would be in twenty years time, and he continued to stare with amazement.

'Take your time in having your fill, Roman!' Macha spat up at him.

He blinked, still speechless, as his mind revolved. So Jodocca could not be here, but surely she was not far away?

'What's your name, woman?'

She drew herself up proudly. 'I am Macha,

head of this vill and who in Hades do you think you arrogant Romans are to cone in here stamping through our homes, and then having the nerve to steal the oat cakes I had just baked!'

So that was it, Marcus thought, and he could not help but grin. 'Were they good ones?'

The question flat-footed Macha, as he had intended. 'None of your business!'

'I'd like one!' he asked softly, turning on his well practised little-boy-lost look.

'Get stuffed!' Macha spat at him.

'Please!' he insisted nicely.

Macha did not know what to do. They were the centre of everyone's eyes, and especially those of the elders. The Roman soldiers had gathered nearby, another officer amused and absorbed by this side play.

'I'll pay!' Marcus hastened to add.

'I would put poison in them first!' Macha retorted.

'Well, in that case Rome would lose a good officer,' he drawled, intent on flat-footing her all the time. He slowly dismounted, aware that Crispus frowned at this and wondered whether his officer had gone stark raving mad.

Marcus threw the woman a pert, challenging look and stepped into her hut. Macha seethed with anger at this Roman. She was upset because Jodocca had left at last, and she had no one really to talk to. With her temper at high pitch she stormed after him.

'I meant what I said,' Marcus told her, and jingled some coins. By all the gods, he thought, the inside was even more primitive. There were a few basic pieces of furniture, carved from wood in the form of rather crude stools. One small bench, two truckle-type beds, and that was all. No other furnishings, no insulation against the cold and a miserable cooking fire. There was not one object classed as aesthetic. Yet this could not mean Britons lacked the culture, because the artwork in their torques was superb.

Macha snatched two oatcakes, thrust them at him and ignored his money. 'What's your game, Roman?'

Marcus bit into the cake. Why, it was delicious! And to think it was made on this primitive fire. He marvelled and took his time eating, then licked up each finger crumb before he answered. He had already decided to take the bull by the horns.

'I am in love with your daughter, Jodocca!' he told her in a low voice.

Now it was Macha's turn to be shocked. Her eyes opened wide as she studied him. They went from head to toe and slowly travelled back again, and she gave the tiniest nod to herself. No wonder her daughter had been so smitten. This one was all man—but he was still Roman. Yet, trying to be fair, she could not think of another Briton with the same superb physical presence and intelligent power of mind. If Jodocca did marry for a second time, this was the kind of man for her. He would control her, firmly yet fairly, and she would respect him. As he stared down at her she felt mesmerised by his powerful personality, and she was more impressed than she knew she dared show.

'So?' she grunted in reply, her thoughts spinning in all directions.

'I want her as my wife,' Marcus continued implacably, 'but she won't say yes and she won't say no! You are her mother, what should I do?' he asked reasonably and hopefully.

Macha half turned away, then looked back and up at him again. 'Don't ask me,' she said wryly. 'I'm just her mother. Jodocca does what she wants, when she wants, and devil take the hindermost.'

Marcus nodded half to himself. 'No influence anywhere?'

Macha shook her head sadly. 'Only one old man, her grandfather might have had influence, but he's not around now.'

'She's not here, so where is she?'

Macha stiffened. 'I don't know and if I did I would not tell you, Roman!'

Marcus believed her, and he nodded to himself. 'So I'll just have to be patient and wait!'

Macha frowned. 'Wait?'

'Until just before winter—she said she would give me her answer then,' Marcus explained, and he saw Jodocca's mother was surprised.

'What do they call you and what is your rank?' Macha wanted to know, curious.

Marcus told her quite frankly, only holding back sensitive and secret information. There was something about the woman he liked, and not just because she was Jodocca's mother. She was a fine and well made female, with withheld energy and dynamic power. A second thought entered his head. He rolled it around in his mind for a few seconds and grinned. Perfect!

'What's so funny now?' Macha demanded to know, sensing the change of mood.

'I'll leave you now,' Marcus told her. 'I shall be away for a bit,' he said smoothly, 'but I'll be back at the agreed time for your daughter's answer, here at this vill.' He turned and stepped back, lightly catching her arm. 'Stay inside, will you?' he asked mischievously. 'There is someone outside who wants to meet you.'

Macha scowled. What was his game now? 'Don't play pranks on me, Roman!' she spat at him. 'I know exactly who is out there and why!'

'Not this time you don't!' He chuckled and strode from her hut, leaving her deeply puzzled.

Outside, the men were all attention, and Marcus spotted Sellus, then beckoned him over.

'Sir?'

Marcus moved nearer, so his words could not be overheard. 'Inside that hut is a fine, upstanding woman but she has one hell of a temper. She might just be what you're looking for!' he hinted as his eyes twinkled.

Sellus studied him. Surely this officer would not jest? Marcus realised his predicament. 'I mean it. If you intend to take your discharge in the area this is indeed a good place and that woman in there is your age group and as tough as nails. I'll tell you something else. I bet she'd be good in bed as well! Over to you, soldier!' he grinned. 'Return at your leisure!' he said in a loud voice, and frowned a warning at Crispus.

Grinning wildly, Marcus vaulted onto his horse and edged over to Crispus. 'I'll explain later! Venus is hovering in his heart though I think that the soldier's rites of passage might get a bit rocky at times!'

Sellus eyed the hut again without hesitation or preamble, then strode inside as it was his right. Macha jumped. She had been lost in a brown study at the realisation and knowledge of who the officer was. Jodocca had chosen well this time. Yet, how could she hope to have a life with him? It was not just the cultural and political clash, it was the

68

impracticability of the situation in general. She never heard Sellus enter, and in took her a few seconds to realise she was no longer alone.

'Who are you? What do you think you're doing here? This is my private home! Get out, Roman!' she snarled at Sellus.

He ignored her while he examined her body carefully. My! His officer was correct. This was a well fleshed woman with ample hips, lovely big breasts, and a not unhandsome face with two blue eyes that blazed fury. She was just his type in shape, perfect in height and weight. He walked forward and daringly prodded her rump with one hand.

Macha whipped round and, with a balled fist, let drive. It hit him flush on the jaw. He staggered backwards, but as one hand went to feel his hurt he beamed with delight. She certainly had the temper and strength to go with it. He nodded sagely to himself.

'I like you,' he confided calmly, his eyes glowing with admiration.

Macha took a deep breath and grabbed a short hunting spear. 'Get out of here before I run you through, Roman!' She snarled.

Sellus beamed his approval. 'You have spirit, my good woman and—'

'I am not your good woman, Roman, but I'll certainly make you a dead man if you don't get out this instant!' she shouted as her temper exploded and she jabbed with her spear.

Sellus smartly side-stepped the blow, and decided it might be more prudent to let matters rest for the time being. He looked at her red face, the grim mouth. 'I'll be back!' he promised. 'Because I think you are lovely. You will be perfect to me in bed, and we'll have some great fun together. I am taking an honourable discharge, and I intend to settle in the area. I'd planned to marry, and I have been looking for a long time. We will make a splendid couple. You may not know this yet, but I will give you plenty of time to think about it!' he ended, then strode to his horse and mounted.

Macha was speechless. Just who did he think he was? It was like a nightmare. The Romans clattered away, and with their disappearance the Britons relaxed, and a few of them clustered around her home. Some of them grinned at her, which meant they had heard every word.

'And you can all wipe those silly smirks off your faces!' she grated, eyes narrow with humiliation and wrath. She went on the attack. 'And if you lot don't have something better to do, I could well remedy the situation. This vill is nothing but a tip of disgust. It stinks, to start with, so you can all begin to help me clean up.'

FIVE

Jodocca rode at a gentle pace, half the time lost in complicated thoughts. She felt utterly miserable at leaving her Roman and her home, then she honestly asked herself how could he ever be her Roman? Their situation was just about impossible. Even dear Lud had refused to give her a straight answer, which could only mean he must have no idea either.

Bran rode ahead, in his favourite place at point. Riothamus was one-horse length behind her, while at her immediate rear rode Kei and Verica. Her other men brought up the last point yet no one spoke. She was still unenthusiastic about Verica, because she was a silent little thing, absolutely hopeless with weapons. She had nothing to say for herself, so would obviously be a boring drag.

Kei was another matter entirely. He was so young and active he could slip through the country like a shadow, and she berated herself for not having thought about him before. Already he had proved his worth, because he kept darting out to their flanks, checking them, and it was he who had brought the news that a detachment of Romans was also on the march. It was obvious they were heading for Gloucester, so prudently the Britons kept to all of their old trails. It would be very foolish

71

to be on a Roman road with legionnaires about.

Riothamus rode up. 'Where to, Lady?'

Jodocca was annoyed with him. He knew perfectly well where they were heading. He was just trying to force his attention on her, but she bit her tongue. 'We're riding up north but around Gloucester. There are just too many of us now to be a trading party especially without trade goods. There is no great need for hurry and I want to keep the horses fresh for an emergency. I want to call in and check on Lud, if he hasn't already left.'

Riothamus frowned. 'Is that wise, Lady? He will have left his old place and have gone to the next nemed.'

Jodocca ignored this. She gave the orders and made the decisions, and, even if Lud had left, she knew the locality of the next nemed. 'We will cold-camp tonight and I want to stop early, because I have a lot of thinking to do and I do not want to be interrupted by anyone!' and she stared at her bodyguard firmly. Riothamus had the grace to break eye contact first, sensing this was not a good time to press himself forward on her.

They cold camped, while there was still daylight left and Kei returned after only a short ride to give details of the Romans' location. To her surprise, they had also camped and immediately she understood why. They were not all fit fighting men. She wondered who was in charge.

Verica picked up a spear. She felt lost and miserable, because it was obvious this was not going to work out as she had hoped. Jodocca had barely exchanged a word with her, and her son, thriving on the responsibility of being a roving lookout, seemed hardly at her side. She felt so alone and was acutely conscious that, when it came to fighting, she was just about useless. If only they were travelling by chariot, how she would then shine.

She strolled down a trail. The men would arrange a meal, but it would be nice to find some fresh nettles for when Jodocca did give permission for a fire to be lit. She could carry them bundled on the side of her saddle. Fresh green food was always so vital after a winter to help against the gum rot, which always happened when they went for a long period without green food.

Her path went almost straight, then veered sharply to one side, where the animals had all automatically turned to avoid a small stand of trees. Without bothering to look ahead, she strolled down it. The bear was big, male and bad-tempered. It had just gone through a hard winter and had awoken from hibernation with the most terrible hunger. The last thing he was prepared to tolerate was a human wandering into his territory. He gave one vicious growl and charged.

Verica had no time either to shout, move or

throw her spear. She stood frozen as death charged at her. There was a violent crash on her right and a man leaped into view. Verica stifled a scream of shock as the man lifted his javelin, aimed carefully, then lunged skilfully and accurately into the bear's heart. It reared up, clawed wildly at the javelin, then slowly tilted over and crashed on the path.

The man stepped back, retrieved the javelin, wiped the blade on a handful of grass, then turned towards her. Verica gave another gasp—he was a Roman! One hand shot to her mouth in fresh alarm, but he said something to her in a gentle voice then slowly lowered his hands placatingly.

She understood in a flash because Verica was a lot brighter than many people realised, Jodocca included. He had no Dubonnii words. Yet he had saved her life. 'Jodocca!' she shouted frantically. Were there other enemies about? She nearly went into a panic, then stopped to study him carefully. He was incredibly dirty, his leather armour had twigs caught in it here and there and he looked thoroughly dishevelled as well as hungry. He had been living rough, which meant he was a deserter from Rome. Was this good or bad?

Jodocca, Riothamus and the rest of the little group thundered down to where the two stood. Riothamus automatically lifted his spear to kill an enemy.

'No!' Verica screeched. 'He saved my life

from that bear!'

Jodocca weighed up the general situation in a flash and she glowered a warning at Riothamus. She studied the Roman. 'Who are you? What are you doing here?' she questioned, but immediately understood as he shook both shoulders. She switched to Latin and saw relief flood his eyes.

'I have deserted, Lady!' Platon told her quickly. Thank Zeus they could communicate. He did not like the look of the man with the spear who wore such a hostile look on his face, yet he knew instinctively the lady was the leader, which he found strange, but somehow acceptable. 'I became totally fed up with my life as a soldier!'

Jodocca's eyebrows shot up. 'Wasn't that rather a dangerous thing to do!' she asked coolly. What kind of a trap was this? Surely Marcus could not be at the back of this-or could he? Then her commonsense told her this was out of the question for a man stationed at the fort.

Platon felt desperate. How could he impress her enough to be allowed to live? 'Yes, my Lady. If they catch me it will be a pretty horrible death.'

Jodocca stared hard into his eyes, wary, suspicious and working out all possible permutations. There was something open, honest and frank, almost appealing about him, and she reviewed the general situation. He had not known they were coming this way, and she threw a look at Verica. She looked at the bear's body and noted what a good clean kill it had been. Trust stupid Verica to wander down a path without looking for danger first—and she scowled at her. This man, though, had saved her life and done it most efficiently. He was a very highly trained warrior, and those like him were always wanted but how far could he be trusted?

'Exactly why?' she demanded to know.

Platon lifted both hands and eloquently began: 'I hate Rome now, and loathe the life of one of her soldiers. I want to make a new life for myself. I don't want to be a Roman anymore. I would like to become a Briton. I am a good fighter, I know how Roman officers think. I know their strategy and tactics. I think I could help you.'

Jodocca acknowledged these very good points. 'You gave your loyalty to Rome,' she said slowly. 'If we take you in, how long will it be before you turn against us?' she asked bluntly.

Platon closed his eyes a little. She was right to be suspicious. So how could he make her understand he was genuine?

Verica had no Latin, but she could understand their voices' nuances, and, knowing Jodocca as she thought she did, she knew there was suspicion as well as hostility. Riothamus was dangerous too. If the Roman made one move he was a dead man. She studied him and liked what she saw. He was afraid of his current situation, but did not grovel. He held himself proudly as a real man would. Something tugged at her heartstrings, and she stepped forward, rather surprised with herself.

'Jodocca!' she said firmly. 'I owe him my life!'

Jodocca frowned at her. Was it her imagination or had some subtle change come over Verica? Where was the wishy-washy girl now? Verica stood before her, upright, firm, and with eyes almost cold. Was it possible there was more to this girl than met the eye? Then a possible explanation entered her head compounded with a streak of mischief.

'You can come with us, while on trial,' she replied in Latin. 'You will always be with this woman who will start to teach you our language. She is a widow. That boy there is called Kei, and he is her son. If you want to impress me, you will learn our language and adapt to our ways and forget everything that was Roman. After that we'll see. The first sign of breach of trust, and I will personally hound you to your death and that will not be a good one either,' she said coldly. 'Riothamus, he comes with us, and you will not antagonise him either if you wish to stay healthy and breathing. Verica, this man is in your charge. You will report to me every evening, as to how he is progressing with our language. Now all of you go away and let me have some peace and quiet!' she snapped, feeling sudden and unexpected waves of fatigue wash through her. Her life was getting far too complicated. Being a leader was not all that it was cracked up to be. Marcus did have one point, after all. As a Roman wife she would live in the lap of luxury with no problems of any kind. Oh Lud, why didn't you advise me so I could understand your hidden meaning? she groaned to herself as she settled with her back against a tree once more. She simply must talk to Lud again, come what may. Caratacus would have to wait a few more days.

Riothamus eyed her, then withdrew. He had hoped she would invite him to sit with her, and he felt chagrined. There was so much he suddenly wanted to tell her, but again, as in the past, she had erected a mental shield round herself, totally excluding him. He sat down some distance away from the little group, and moodily started to chew some cold meat. It was tough but on the tasty side. He studied the Roman who sat with Verica. Fancy being lumbered with him. What had come over the lady to contemplate allowing an enemy soldier in their midst? What was all this claptrap about deserting? It sounded a crazy put-up job yet he could find no flaw in what the man had said.

He disliked him though. With that instant

spur-of-the-moment hostility, which is natural, yet without logical reason, he glowered at him, and Verica did not miss this. She lifted her head, jutted her jaw and held hard eye contact until Riothamus was forced to look away first.

'He doesn't like me,' Platon said, then realised the girl did not understand him. He closed his eyes and allowed his shoulders to sag with a weariness that was not feigned. Bolting and deserting were all very well but when it came down to the nitty-gritty, it was a lot more difficult than he had realised. To start with, superb fighting soldier as he was, he had discovered to his humiliation that catching game on which to live was beyond him. It had not been for lack of trying either. It had only dawned upon him slowly that he lacked the necessary skills for tracking and stalking. Since his run, his belly had become flatter and flatter with hunger pains. Now to sit here, in an almost companionable silence even with men who hated him, he felt a huge weight slide from his shoulders.

Tomorrow was another day. Dare he hope that it would be day one of a new life? He surreptitiously eyed the girl by his side, who had given him some wonderful dried meat. He guessed she was roughly his own age. She was warm and not polished or even clean, but still wholesome and very attractive. He sniffed and caught the scent of some pungent herbs, which she must have picked to rub on her skin. This bouquet was tantalisingly attractive to his nostrils and he threw her a gentle smile.

Verica examined him and smiled in return. She felt incredibly at peace. This Roman, this hated enemy was bound with her in the great chain forged when one owed life to the other. Her eyes gave him a detailed appraisal, and she liked what she saw. He was not exactly handsome, as Verica understood the word, but he had a fascinating air about him, which attracted her.

Suddenly, he grinned openly and winked. Instantly, she burst into a low, throaty laugh. Placing her right hand on her breast, she said her name and made him repeat it until he pronounced it with the correct vocal inflection.

Jodocca missed nothing at all. She had noted the blatant hostility from her personal bodyguard, which annoyed her. She noted the Roman grin at Verica and was amused at his wink. Verica's laugh was uplifting and lightened the general atmosphere. Had she been wise to put these two together? But it was done now, for better or worse.

They were up at dawn, and Jodocca eyed the sky to calculate the weather. It would be a good day later on once the mist had lifted. She called the group around. 'Bran, go off and scout for us again. I wish to be informed exactly where those marching Romans are. Kei, I want you to ride and see if Lud and Osa have left and if so track them for a bit for me to confirm they are heading for the next nemed. I wish to see Lud again before we go up to Caratacus.'

Riothamus did not like any of this. A lot of unnecessary fuss was made about this old Druid, which he considered totally unnecessary. He was one of the few Britons who had scant regard for Druids as a whole. He considered them leeches on society, and much as he hated Rome, he did agree they should be exterminated.

* * *

Marcus also did not hurry. With Crispus on his left flank, they rode their horses at a walk, which gave ample time to look around and study the land. They rode on their splendid road, with Marcus in deep thought. Then he made his decision. He turned and gave Crispus a frank look.

'I haven't gone mad,' he said slowly, opening the conversation ball.

Crispus gave a snort, which could have meant anything. He had left the conversation opening to his officer to start, which would indicate rank had vanished.

'You could have fooled me,' he drawled slowly. 'What exactly is going on, sir?'

Marcus came out with a rush of words. 'I have fallen head over heels in love with a

81

Briton,' he started, then explained in very great detail.

Crispus heard him out in silence. This was something that had never entered his head. He would not have believed it from anyone else either. Frowning a little, he considered as Marcus finished and awaited his companion's reaction.

'I think you might just be biting off a little more then you can chew,' he warned gravely. 'As well bed with a she bear!' he added dryly.

Marcus grinned: 'I'll have to take that chance,' he replied, then explained about Sellus.

Crispus snorted with derision. 'Surely to Zeus, a man can do his own matchmaking.'

'True, but a little gentle shove does no harm, and a man going there all the time can keep us fully informed on the quiet,' and he gave a wolfish grin.

Crispus smiled at this and nodded sagely. It was a clever ploy, and one that could only be played with the right participants. Sellus and this Macha would do nicely. 'Clever!' he congratulated his companion.

Marcus eyed him. 'What do you think about me though?' he asked very anxiously.

Crispus took his time in answering, as there were more permutations here than met the eye at first glance. It was a complicated situation for which there was no clear affirmative or negative. Love was a strange emotion. He, thank all the gods, had never suffered this affliction. He just used any available whore when necessary. The very idea of tying himself to one person for many, many years was not his idea of fun. People changed as they grew older. So did their moods. On the other hand, some men and women could suffer incredible loneliness without a permanent mate. Was Marcus one? He suspected that might be possible. Crispus knew he was totally exempt. He gave a heavy sigh, and threw a keen look at his younger companion.

'It might work,' he said cautiously, 'but you will have some almighty problems. First of all, that of the total occupation of Britain, and secondly, I simply do not see how the lady, as you describe her, could be turned into a Roman. There will be religious clashes to start with, to say nothing of disagreements over culture. Will constant bickering make a happily married life? Rather you than me!'

Marcus scowled at him. 'You could give me a little more hope!'

'You wanted the truth, didn't you?' Crispus retorted evenly. 'Just how do you propose to win her to your point of view when everyone knows much blood will soon be spilled and most of it is going to be British? Furthermore, you would have to resign your rank and leave the legion so exactly how would you pass your days? Twiddling your thumbs?'

Marcus felt his heart sink. 'Love is supposed to conquer all,' he grumbled.

Crispus had a sudden thought. 'Breed horses,' he muttered more to himself, then he gave a sagacious nod. 'That would keep you well and truly occupied, it would suit your temperament, and with luck, suit your wild British lady!'

Marcus brightened. Why hadn't he thought of that? The idea was brilliant. The British native stock of animals was basically sound, and, with judicious breeding, he could develop an excellent strain of riding and pack horse, which would always be in demand. His heart lightened, because he knew his companion was very accurate. With nothing positive to do he would be like a bear with a sore head.

'Splendid!' he complimented Crispus again.

'There's only one snag,' Crispus pointed out, calmly.

'What's that?'

Crispus grinned. 'First catch, then win your lady—and with open warfare in the offing!' Then he changed the subject. It had been thrashed out long enough. 'We are catching up with our men. I can see their dust ahead,' and he reverted back to the position of rank. 'There is the matter of that deserter to deal with, sir.'

Marcus's jaw set. 'Yes!' he said grimly. 'We have to catch him for the sake of discipline and make an example out of him just in case any others of that maniple also get stupid ideas.'

Crispus felt anger rise. A deserter was a total disgrace to any legion. 'I had had quite a bit of trouble with him for a while so had Marius, but I never thought he'd do a runner. I hope by now the British have found him and run him through. It would save us the job.'

Marcus nodded as he pushed into a canter, and swung aside to pass the rear troops, Crispus followed briskly. Shortly, they reached the van and Marcus met the tribune, who joined him, while Crispus vanished to ferret around and see if all met his exactingly high standards.

'All is well, sir!' the tribune told him. 'have the usual scouts out, and I'm using the auxiliaries more now, but we have flushed no game,' he said, meaning Britons. 'I let the auxiliaries run free every morning, on their own at times, now I know there are no natives around. It is good exercise and good experience for them.'

Marcus was not so sure about this. Some of the auxiliaries, especially men born in wild savage countries, were not always controllable when let loose to hunt on their own. But if there were no Britons around, which seemed to be the case, little harm could be done.

'We will camp early tonight, and leave just after the dawn,' Marcus ordered. What he would really like to do was a fast and forced march to wake up these men, some of whom were somewhat sluggish, but this was not possible with all of them. Splitting his force would be too dangerous to contemplate when in enemy territory.

He eyed the sky. It had been a delightful day and one in which he felt empathy with the island. There was no roasting sun, like over Rome, this was more a gentle heat, and the greenery was pleasing to the eye. It was true the cold months here could be horrendous, but with the proper building and the right plumbing life could be made very comfortable indeed. Quite a number of retired soldiers were happy to live in Britain, so why not he? This reasoning brought Jodocca back to his mind again. There had to be something that would attract her, but wrack his brains as he might, no good bait sprang to mind. 'I won't be beaten!' he told himself. 'I'm just not thinking straight. The day I finish this commission my discharge request will follow,' he vowed.

SIX

Jodocca knew the tears were streaming down her dirty cheeks, and she cried her grief aloud. She stood slightly apart from the rest of the shocked group, as her mind reeled with horror. Very few bodies looked good in death, but these two were so shocking it all seemed unreal.

Riothamus approached her warily, and with considerable trepidation. He dared to reach out and gently touch her shoulder, his own eyes flaring with his shock. Jodocca looked around, seeing the huddled people equally disbelieving.Verica cried and though Kei struggled to be manful he did not quite succeed.

The Roman stood uneasily to one side, not quite knowing what to do or where to put himself. He felt the waves of fresh hostility and held himself ready for anything. Then Verica, sniffing loudly, reached and slid her hand into his. Platon licked very dry lips and hesitated, while he kept a watchful eye on the lady leader. He was as appalled as the Britons but his mind had started to work rapidly.

Jodocca forced herself to be in control and strode over to him. 'Why?' she demanded to know. 'Why, damn you? You are a Roman—why?' she shouted, and now her voice had a tinge of hysteria.

Platon gulped and shook his head, miserably. 'There has been an edict against all Druids, but not this!' And he shook his head. 'Not like this, Lady!'

'Two frail old men in the evening of their lives!' Jodocca ranted as her grief began to turn to rage, and she became the more dangerous for it. 'Look at them!' she stormed. Platon did, and his shoulders slumped. They had not been killed cleanly. It was true one of them had received a javelin thrust to his throat but the other, the Druid, had been stamped to death. It was as if a mad animal had killed him.

'Rome would not agree with this,' he told her firmly, but still prudently watched all the rest of the warriors.

Jodocca turned away from him. She knew a good leader did not take rage out on one of lower rank without good reason, yet she boiled now. She was not far off going berserk. It was Kei who had told them. He had ridden back to them, at manic speed, almost incoherent with his own shock. He had ridden so fast he had collided with Jodocca's horse and for a short period there had been a tangled confusion of rearing horses, plus squeals of equine anger.

'Kei!' Jodocca had gone to rebuke him for such wild riding, then one glimpse at his staring, white-rimmed eyes had warned her of some kind of emergency. The boy had been beyond coherent explanation, so they had just ridden off at an angle to the nemed and made their own ghastly discovery.

The two old men had never left the little place to start their travels north. She realised it was only a short time ago she had been here herself to talk and confide with Lud. Osa had obviously died first, struggling to protect his Druid with his pathetic little weapon, then it had been Lud's turn. He had died as badly as anyone could. It was simple to see who done the killing. Apart from the brutal marks on his frail body, there were boot prints everywhere, Roman boot prints.

Jodocca struggled to regain her wits and tried to work out a timescale. Riothamus stood nearby hesitantly, his glaring face on Platon. 'Lady, shall we bury them here as it is a holy glade?' He did not like the look on her face. It was too far to go back with the bodies to their vill and though he had known the lady was fond of the old Druid, he had not expected this outward show of genuine grief. After all, although the old man had died badly he had only been a Druid. No one of consequence in his mind.

Jodocca shook her head fiercely. 'No! I will not have my beloved grandfather thrust in a grave unavenged!'

Riothamus staggered with shock, and the others within earshot were also shaken. 'Your grandfather?' the bodyguard asked. 'I did not know! I had no idea!'

Jodocca snarled at him. 'Why should you? It was not your business, but it was mine and my mother's. Someone is going to pay for this. I'll see blood spilled if it's the last thing I do!'

Riothamus's mind had almost gone blank with shock, and he knew he would have to think about all this later. What exactly did the lady intend to do? He did not like the look in her eyes and the set of her jaw.

'Lady!' Platon said a little nervously. 'I was here, just after I deserted. I blundered into this clearing and met the two oldsters. I bowed my head to them in respect, and that one,' and he pointed to Lud's battered body, 'smiled at me, and his eyes seemed to go right through me, with enormous wisdom. We had no words yet, I sensed in a flash he knew all there was to know about me. He shook his head and waved his hand around here and I knew he meant I could not stay. Then, he waved and pointed to one side, and I ran off on the trail he indicated.'

'When exactly was this, can you remember accurately?' Jodocca shot at him.

Platon frowned, aware of the importance of the question. 'I think it would be two dawns ago but I had become so hungry and worried the last couple of days are very confused.'

Jodocca beckoned to Bran. 'How far away are those marching Romans?'

'Quite near, Lady, really. They are not moving with their usual speed. That officer is leading them again.'

'What!' Jodocca almost spat out the word with shock. She had presumed Marcus was still at the Fort. She turned back to Platon. 'Who exactly would do something like this?'

Platon gulped. 'It could be any man, sent

90

out by himself as a scout. If when they returned and explained what they had done it would not be held against them, because of the general edict to kill all Druids and finish off their religion. Though not like this,' he added hastily. 'Both old men should have gone with a javelin thrust, clean and quick.'

Jodocca nodded to herself. These words rang true and she was astute enough to understand how this Roman must feel. 'Make two litters!' she ordered. 'Wrap the bodies in spare cloaks!'

Riothamus walked up, ignoring the Roman. 'Lady, what can I do? I so want to help you,' and his tone was gentle and appealing, lacking its usual bombast.

Jodocca turned to him as Platon stood aside. Her heart had broken. She knew that and also she writhed at her crass stupidity. How right Macha had been to pour scorn on her love plans. The Roman had made an utter fool of her and she gritted her teeth with anger. She had allowed herself to be bewitched with handsome looks and masculine power. All a façade. While here, before her was a true Briton. A proven warrior whom she had always ignored. How stupid could she be? She looked into the eyes of Riothamus and saw genuine concern for the first time. She would never be fooled again, she vowed to herself, and now was neither the time nor the place to think of heart and love matters. Later, when they had beaten the Romans, she could review this situation: right now, she wanted nothing but vengeance.

'There is something you can do for me personally,' she said quietly.

'Anything!' and Riothamus meant it.

'I have some writing parchment somewhere. I am going to write a message. Can you then wrap it around a stone and hurl it into that Roman night camp for me?'

He frowned, bewildered, but nodded a quick assent. Jodocca hastened to explain. 'I want the man who did this handed over to me for open, personal battle before my people and the Romans themselves.'

'I would be proud to fight for you, Lady!' Riothamus said quickly.

Jodocca shook her head. 'Thank you Riothamus but this is very personal to me. Lud—was—my grandfather!' she pointed out.

Platon strode back to join them and butt in. 'Lady, I could not help but overhear. Let me have that honour!'

'You?' sneered Riothamus.

Platon swung around to face him, vibrating cold fury. 'The Lady runs matters here, not you, big mouth!' he snarled. 'You just fancy yourself. You wouldn't last a week under legion discipline! Nothing but a bag of wind and piss!' he jeered.

Riothamus went scarlet and prepared to

lunge forward. Hastily Jodocca thrust herself between both of them. 'Enough!' she growled. She eyed Platon. 'But you are a deserter,' she reminded him.

Platon nodded. 'Arrange appropriate truce terms,' he told her. 'Who is better to fight a Roman than another Roman?' he asked reasonably. He held his breath. If she would agree and he won, these Britons would truly accept him. He would sort out the other one another day because his instinct told him both Verica and Kei would watch his back against treachery from Riothanius.

Jodocca wrote thoughtfully with her own blood from a pricked finger. It was crude but there was nothing else to hand and it seemed appropriate. It was only a small piece of finely tanned skin but it served. Then she eyed the hastily constructed litters with the pathetic bodies wrapped up well in robes. A few of them might go cold tonight but poor Lud was cold forever.

She gave the writing to Riothamus who, with great care, wrapped it around a hefty-sized stone. Then she beckoned to Bran. 'Ride back to the vill. Explain what has happened and exactly what I plan to take place. Take an escort. If you meet Romans, do not fight. Bolt! Riothamus you have an escort also. We will await here.'

She placed sentries, then realised she had used up her manpower so she placed herself on a lookout rota.

'Platon, have you any idea at all who might have done this?'

He shook his head unhappily. 'I would suspect an auxiliary as some of then are barely civilised when let loose,' he explained. 'That's why Rome makes them wait so long for citizenship. It's when they go out to forage or as lone scouts. They all know of the edict to kill Druids and some thrive on killing. That's why they make good fighters.'

'And good butchers!' Jodocca grated.

Platon felt strung up with his nerves in tatters. What happened in the next twenty-four hours would decide the remainder of his life. He gave a limp grin at Verica and Kei, and she squeezed his hand encouragingly in return while Kei threw him a frank smile. He liked this Roman and hoped he was going to stay. If he did, would his wonderful mother marry him?

It was Riothamus who returned first. 'No problems, Lady,' he reassured her. 'They had scouts out of course but making enough noise to frighten the game everywhere. I dodged them, hid my horse, slithered to a good position and hurled the stone easily inside their night camp. It landed near a sentry who picked it up, opened it, then took it into a tent. An officer soon came out to question him and look around.'

'A big man wearing bronze greaves in his

mid-twenties?' Jodocca checked quickly.

Riothamus nodded and again wondered. There was definitely something going on and he knew he would have to think about this later.

Bran returned next. 'I peeped at the enemy camp quickly. There is activity and I saw one of their leaders mount up and with an escort move away from their camp's boundaries.'

Jodocca mounted quickly. She waved her hand and a few of them moved to carry the litters. 'It's not long to dark, Lady!' Riothamus pointed out.

Jodocca ignored this and, with herself at their head, they moved very slowly to where she now knew the Romans must appear. Platon wisely kept to the rear to hide his identity until it became useful. It did not take them long though Riothamus had begun to have palpitations. They were heavily outnumbered and he prayed to the gods that the lady knew what she was doing.

She rode her horse from a small clump of trees. As she studied Marcus Gaius again she felt something very bitter and acid enter her throat and she spat. To think she had ever dared to consider matrimony with him. It flashed through her mind that perhaps she would never marry again but remain always their single, unattached leader until she became too old.

She had ordered Riothamus to keep away

but it had taken a hard glower to enforce this demand. As she rode into view so did Marcus push his horse forward alone. It was wonderful to see her again yet he sensed there was something very badly wrong. The look in her eyes was murderous and he was totally bewildered.

'You asked for a short truce on a personal matter!' he said stiffly while his heart thumped with worry. What in Hades had come over her? What had he done, for Zeus's sake? His escort waited uneasily a few horse lengths to his rear while the camp stood at full alert.

Jodocca glowered at him, then turned on her horse as the two litters were carried carefully down to the pair of them. 'Our Druid has been killed,' she grated at him, 'and none of us like the way it was done, Roman. I didn't think even vile Romans could stoop quite so low!'

Marcus was taken aback. 'What do you mean?' he snapped, feeling his own temper start to rise.

Jodocca could have screamed her fury at him. Did he think she was stupid? With a huge effort she kept herself under tight control. The men bearing the litters approached.

Marcus went rigid as he heard Crispus fidget so he half turned and scowled warningly at him. The four Britons reached their leader and respectfully lowered the litters to the ground.

'Uncover them!' Jodocca barked. 'Now, Roman! Take a long, hard look at what you brave Romans do to the aged and frail. Look at those boot marks. Roman boots! So are you going to tell me Rome approves of ancients being stamped to death? Especially my beloved grandfather?' and her tone was acid.

Marcus was more deeply shocked than he showed. No, Rome would not approve of this one bit! Druid or no Druid. There were more civilised ways to kill, gladiatorial contests, battle, executions like crucifixions—not this. He took his time and let his eyes rove over the two corpses. And one was her beloved grandfather? This was bad indeed. Very bad.

The boot marks were plain on the old man's flesh. His robe had been torn and his ribs broken. He flared his nostrils with fury. Some man had done a bad day's work here. These people revered their Druids and such a bestial death would never be forgiven. He alone knew that Scapula was preparing to issue an edict against the Silures tribe over the Severn. All males over twelve years were to be exterminated and all females enslaved. He thought this was crazy enough but these old men's deaths would inflame the tribes even more. There could well be a general uprising. There was enough trouble in the east from their Queen Boudicca. This could be the final straw to put the whole of Britain in open revolt. It was true they had four good legions spread throughout the island but would they be enough to cope with a general uprising? He had grave reservations. Scapula had to be informed immediately. Right here and now he had to find a wild killer. It could only be an auxiliary, he sensed.

What appalled him most of all was that it was her relative. Now he understood the hate that filled his beloved's eyes. He felt sick at heart and nodded to Crispus to move his horse nearer so he could see more plainly.

Jodocca spoke each word like an icicle. 'If you look at his hands you will see skin under his nails. He tried to fight back. Your heroic man will be marked.'

Marcus saw she was correct. This would help with identification at least. He opened his mouth but she forestalled him. 'I want this man!' she grated. 'I want British justice!'

Marcus knew he was in a cleft stick. He could think of nothing but how beautiful she looked in her rage. A hatred which flooded from her in waves. He knew that whatever there might have been between them had well and truly vanished. He felt sick to the depth of his guts.

'What would that be?' he asked quietly, playing for time.

'He will be brought here to be killed before my people. Oh don't worry your hypercritical Roman heart. It will not be a public execution.

It will be a one-to-one fight with a truce guaranteed between our two forces. The victor to go free. Untouched by either side,' she challenged.

Marcus considered this. It would be highly unusual and normally utterly impossible but such circumstances as these were not written in any Roman warfare manual. On the other hand, Scapula might be able to make political capital out of such a situation but who would fight for them? Not her, surely? She could never be a match for a highly trained and hardened soldier.

'I agree!' he managed to get out at last but his heart thumped. 'And the victor goes free and unharmed. I swear this on Rome's honour.'

'I too swear if your man is victor not one Briton will lift a hand against him—but you'd be wise to get him off our land!' she warned so all could hear her.

'Give me twenty-four hours to find him and I also vow none of you will be touched if you camp nearby!' he nodded. 'I have a lot of men to check,' he explained.

'We will camp among those trees,' and she pointed to them, knowing they would have a tight guard out in case of more Roman treachery.

Marcus turned and in a cold rage rode back to his men with a silent Crispus one horse length to the rear. Before he entered his tent, he turned to Crispus and spoke in a loud voice, which everyone could not fail to hear.

'I want this camp searched. Every man is to be examined by you in person. When you find him bring him to me. I don't care how you do it, nor how long it takes but until he is found, every man stands at attention. They will not move, eat, drink, piss or crap if they have to stand there all night, and that goes for officers too. Only you and me are exempt. Now see to it!' he said harshly.

He entered his tent and with bowed head leaned against the central support pole. Was it only such a short time ago, he had ridden with Crispus and confided what was in his heart? It seemed like months, even years, and now it was all gone, because of one of his own men. He writhed with rage. He would like to kill the man himself, but Jodocca did have right on her side. He took a deep breath and let out a heavy sigh. She knew perfectly well that good fighters though the Britons were it was most unlikely they would have one competent enough to beat a Roman in hand-to-hand fight. One thing was for sure he told himself, when the Roman soldier won, he would then deal with him in his own way.

He felt something hard and cold in his belly. It went down to his bowels, and he was as miserable as he had ever been in his whole life.

*　　*　　*

That night in a quiet little spot under an oak tree Jodocca and her team buried the two old men. She became all-female again as enough tears flowed to flood a plain. They were all sunk in acute misery, except Platon who was totally detached because of his birth and new position. All he could think about was whom would he be facing? He wished he knew right now, so he could work out appropriate tactics. It was a long time before he dropped off into a rather restless doze, Verica and Kei nearby.

He was up by the dawn with the rest of them, and Jodocca beckoned him over. The other members of the group crowded around in a half circle. Platon felt a wave of unease fill him. What was going to happen now? His heart fluttered with palpitations.

Jodocca sensed this and threw him a wan smile. 'You say you want to be a Briton?'

Platon nodded quickly. He certainly did, more he wanted to wed one but he knew this was neither the time nor the place.

'Very well,' Jodocca said shortly. 'Will you be my official champion and avenge my grandfather's death?'

'I most certainly will,' he vowed realising this was some kind of little ceremony.

'We don't know who he is yet, and you might not be able to beat him?' Jodocca pointed out coolly.

101

Platon's jaw jutted. 'I will be the devil himself to be a Briton and'—he paused to take Verica's hand—'to have this woman's hand in marriage!'

Jodocca was not exactly surprised, because she had felt the empathy and vibes between them even without a common language. She turned to Verica and lifted one eyebrow eloquently. It had not needed an understanding of his speech for Verica to guess his request. She nodded enthusiastically.

Riothamus had been an interested spectator. Everything was moving just a little more quickly than he liked yet he could not fault the lady's plans. How she must now hate Romans, especially that breed of Roman officer. He had finally worked it out to his satisfaction. That arrogant Roman had dared to fancy his lady.

Jodocca gestured with a right hand, and the little half-circle moved even nearer, crowding right up to Platon's back. 'You all know what this is about and who is going to carry our honour for us. As a small council with myself in your head, I pronounce this man is now a Briton and will have the name of Black Raven.' She looked into Platon's eyes. 'In our language, that is Badb Catha so I suggest we Romanise this name, and use the shortened version of Cathus. How do you all vote?'

Platon stood rather uncertainly, a bit uncomfortable at being the focus of all eyes, and he looked helplessly at Verica who gave him a beaming smile and squeezed his hand yet again, while Kei's eyes sparkled. The tiny council finished its brief discussion and chatted freely with enthusiasm, endorsing their approval.

Jodocca was pleased. She had a sudden instinct this was going to be one of her better moves in life. 'From now on, you are no longer Platon, the Roman but Cathus the Briton, and the people of the Dubonnii tribe welcome you with open arms!' It was only a tiny ceremony, because of their circumstances. No mead, no huge feast, and no jollification.

'How do you fight—as a Briton or a Roman?' She wanted to know, it was important.

Cathus replied firmly. 'As a Roman because that is how I have been trained. I will be up against similar. There is no time to train in British tactics.'

Jodocca had suspected this, which made sense. She eyed his javelin and pilum, then studied his dagger before withdrawing her own and offering it to him hilt first. 'Kill him at the end with this if you can. It was my father's, and he was a super fighting chief. May it also bring you luck for our sakes!'

Cathus gave a half bow of politeness, with his head, then examined the knife. He tested the blade for sharpness and the whole weapon for balance. It was a magnificently crafted knife and sharp enough to cut the most flimsy hair. Then it was his turn to surprise the rest of them. He reached inside his tunic and brought forth a hanging medallion, silver-shaped in the outline of a horse's head. It was a beautiful object of very high value.

Cathus grinned at Verica. 'I do not know your matrimonial customs,' he began, 'but I give this to the woman of my choice!' and, stepping forward, he gently placed the long silver chain over Verica's head and neck, and grinned at her with total satisfaction.

Jodocca approved while tears of delight hovered in Verica's eyes and Kei commenced a jig of joy. 'Marriage is a very serious contract with us,' she started. 'A contract freely given between a man and a woman, and we hold both sexes equal in everything. The woman knows she is expected to share all of her husband's fortunes and misfortunes. As long as they both live, she is his equal partner in danger and suffering. Also, we do not have a female dowry!'

Cathus blinked with some surprise and Jodocca smiled at his confusion so she continued. 'It is the man who has to have it! He is supposed to take oxen, horses or other appropriate goods to the woman's parents. For the actual betrothal a medallion is exchanged—which you have done! So what goods can you give to your intended through me? As she has no parents I stand in proxy!'

Cathus was perplexed. He had not expected all of this. Then a grin lit his face. He plunged one hand, under his defensive body armour and it emerged holding a purse, fastened with a drawstring. He shook it, opened it and showed the contents around.

'I don't have as much as I rightly should,' he explained to all of them. 'I was always in trouble, and being fined, but no one knew I had this which I won the only time I ever entered a gambling game!'

Jodocca did some rapid counting, then tipped her head to one side and eyed him with a twinkle. 'I certainly think you have obtained your bride, and I am sure Verica and Kei are proud of you. Do you agree to all this, Verica?'

'Oh I do!'

'Me too!' Kei, added enthusiastically.

Jodocca held both of their hands. 'There can be no proper ceremony and we all know why but by the power vested in me as chief and grand-daughter of a famous Druid, I pronounce these two man and wife!'

There was a burst of good-humoured talk and back-slapping for which Jodocca was grateful. The atmosphere had lightened. Only she still felt so sick at heart and angry and she only half-watched as a crude shelter was built for the couple with one or two earthy jokes. Tomorrow would be a momentous day. She would have to see him again and tears welled up. How cruel life could be. Had Lud suspected something like this?

SEVEN

Jodocca eyed Cathus the next dawn. A careful watch had been kept on the Romans' night camp and they all knew about the soldiers being kept at attention for a long period until there had been sudden activity. There had been enough moonlight for them to see one man detached and, under escort, marched to the officer's tent. What had happened then, they had no idea.

'Do you take your pilum?' Jodocca asked him. She had spent a horrendous night, miserable beyond words compounded with cold rage.

'No, Lady. Javelin and dagger only, provided he is likewise armed,' Cathus confirmed coolly. There were no flutters in him and he knew he was coldly ready to kill or be killed. If the latter he could only hope he had managed to impregnate Verica last night. If not, it certainly would not have been for lack of trying, he mused and she had been more than willing.

'I want you to stay out of sight until they produce their man and march him forward. Then, and only then, show yourself. You will shock them all and it will be an advantage!'

she told him wisely.

Then Kei rushed up, red-faced with excitement. 'Lady, activity from the Romans. A handful of them have stepped forward with a man bound between them.'

'Good!' Jodocca snapped. She looked around. Her scouts had done well. Hidden among the many trees was a huge crowd of her people, come to see justice done. She had given her orders and made sure they were clearly understood. She nodded grimly and gave Cathus another look with elevated eyebrows. He replied with a cool nod while Verica's hands went to her mouth with agitation and Kei hovered from one foot to the other with emotion.

Jodocca rode forward, her horse picking its way delicately. She emerged from the trees and managed to refrain from looking back to check her orders were being obeyed.

Her heart hardened as she saw him again. He sat his horse in the exact spot of the day before. An optio was beside him while two ordinary soldiers held a third between them. He had no joyful smile this time. I should think not, Jodocca told herself.

'And that is your killer?' she asked icily.

'It is he.' Marcus replied with a heavy voice. 'His hands and forearms gave him away. Covered in long scratches and, when challenged, he did not even deny it!'

Jodocca looked into blazing eyes and then

studied the man's body's stance. She knew a tough fighter when she saw one, and, for a fleeting second, a doubt entered her head for Cathus. Could he really take on this one and win? The dice had been thrown though. But this one was arrogant and sure of himself. Not in the least abashed at his current situation. Again a doubt rose but she pushed it firmly aside.

'The weapons will be javelin and dagger only,' she announced.

Marcus felt uneasy. She was just a little too sure of herself. What game did she propose to play? The troops were all on high alert for possible treachery though he guessed her precious oath and honour would not allow this. But what about her followers? Long ago he had taken the time and trouble to understand the British customs. He yearned to speak softly to her but dare not with every ear tuned in their direction to say nothing of her harsh expression.

Crispus sensed his friend's feelings and gritted his teeth. This confounded British female had done something irreparable to Marcus. His eyes were not just cold against their killer but filled with incredible sadness. Would he ever be the same man again? What would he do? Resign? That could take weeks to arrange. Rome could move very slowly at times. Even if he did go, where did that leave Crispus himself? Out on a limb—and alone without someone he considered a brother in arms. He muttered imprecations to himself, suddenly understanding his whole life was on the verge of drastic change. All because of— her.

Jodocca gave him a final harder look, then turned gently and lifted her left hand and arm high and vertical in the air. There was immediate movement to her rear as her people pushed forward through the trees and displayed their vast number.

Marcus was stunned with shock, and he flashed a look at Crispus to see he was equally amazed. So many of them and, taking the female warriors into account with the men, they more than outnumbered the Romans present. He forced his features into a blank mask, while his mind revolved fast. Neither of them had had the faintest idea the British were capable of getting together such a fighting force in this area. He knew the governor had not the slightest idea just as he also knew he would eventually have to ride back with this critical information. From where had they all come? What was most disconcerting of all was their silence. He gritted his teeth and turned his attention to her again.

Jodocca had the advantage now, and she found she could read him easily. She let him sweat a few more seconds before she spoke. 'My people have come to see justice done!'

she explained quietly.

'I see!' Marcus managed to get out though he knew he had broken into a sweat of pure anxiety. He could sense that Crispus was also very much on edge. 'Where is your fighter?' he challenged.

Jodocca now lifted her arm and hand vertically into the air and her champion appeared. Cathus marched toward her purposefully, his eyes fixed rigidly on the auxiliary Marius. *Of course, it would be him!*

An angry growl arose from the watching Romans, as they recognised one who had once been among them. Marcus turned sharply and silenced this noise with a hard look. Deserters might be despised, as indeed they were, but now was not the time and place to demonstrate such scorn.

Marius eyed his deadly rival, and his eyes glowed. How he had loathed this man, and now he could legitimately kill him. Cathus's face showed a similar intent. This was the man who had led him a life of hell, and who, in so many ways, was totally responsible for making him do a runner. This was indeed going to be a very good day, Cathus vowed.

Marcus eyed her. 'Very clever!' he complimented her. 'Set a Roman to catch one!'

Jodocca was quick. 'He is not Roman!' she told him tartly. 'He is the Briton Cathus!' she snapped. 'And our champion against your

110

murderer!'

Marcus saw that Cathus was armed, ready and virtually quivering to start. It crossed his mind to wonder whether there had been bad blood between these two before.

Marius flexed and unflexed his hands and shoulder muscles now that the bindings had been removed from his wrists. He snatched up a dagger and javelin, very eager to fight someone whom he had always despised.

Marcus threw a nod at Jodocca and together they both bellowed, 'Start!'

Both men were bare-headed though each wore the customary Roman body armour. Both were right-handed and their javelins pointed lethally forward as they circled. There was absolute silence from the spectators.

Cathus moved quickly and easily on the balls of his feet, his weight nicely balanced, and he watched Marius through narrowed eyes, ready for any dirty tricks. Both javelins probed experimentally for an opening in the other's defence, seeking a weak spot, and both men covered with adroit sidesteps, then Marius charged in.

For a few seconds Cathus was forced to back-pedal quickly, then he side-slipped, and his javelin prodded. He felt the point enter flesh, but it would only make a minor wound. Marius turned very quickly, for such a large heavy man and he slashed out. Cathus was forced to duck to keep breathing. That had been a wicked blow, but not wholly unexpected in opening fighting rounds.

Marius followed it up with a barrage of savage jabs and again Cathus was forced to retreat to cover. While waiting he had studied the terrain and it was smooth, no bumps to trip the man. He was a little surprised at the savagery from Marius, then it hit him—it was this that the poor old men had faced. Well, he Cathus, a Briton, was no feeble old man. He braked and slashed out to the right. His blade met that of his enemy, and they both clanged, jolting their wrists, then Cathus plunged. He knew he was now faster than ever before in his life. His blade began to dart and peck to right and left. Each time its tip pierced flesh, finding cracks in the other's body armour. Very soon, Marius's leather had began to turn red. And although these were only flesh wounds, not touching anything vital, Cathus knew the blood loss would soon become debilitating.

Cathus leapt sideways and, changing direction completely, he attacked from the other side, while dodging Marius's blade. Marius had started to become confused and perturbed. This was not going exactly as he had planned. It had never entered his head that old Platon could fight to this high standard, and with such speed, and could keep going like this. Although his nostrils flared, his opponent was not breathing heavily at all and for the first time a seed of doubt began to sprout. His concentration slipped for two heartbeats and Cathus sensed this.

Cathus jumped forward frontally, aimed his javelin, then plunged, not for the well-protected heart behind the thick leather padding but for the guts. He felt the javelin's point enter the other's intestines, and he withdrew the blade with a savage twist. He eyed Marius carefully and knew such a wound was quite fatal. He switched hands, put the javelin in his left and with his right pulled out Jodocca's dagger. Then he plunged it forward to where he knew there was a gap in the leather lacing. It entered Marius's heart, and he reared up for a second or two, then slumped down dead.

Cathus sidestepped the corpse, stepped forward as if on parade, and brought the dagger upright in a flourishing salute to his leader. Jodocca gave a little half-bow of her head in an acknowledgement. The Romans stood in stunned and disbelieving silence. Then the watching Britons broke into a roar of triumph.

Marcus eyed them dubiously and shot a warning glance at Crispus, who was on very high alert indeed. Would this now turn into a general battle? Jodocca read their thoughts. How dare they insult her honour and integrity. She turned again, silenced her people with her left hand, then gave a twirling

113

motion with it. Almost like well-drilled soldiers the Britons began to move back into the trees. It was a well disciplined move and Jodocca felt her heart fill with pride. *And up yours, Romans!*

She turned back to look at the officer again. 'There is just one more point,' she began, and she knew her people remained to observe. Withdrawing her own short sword, she rode right up to Marcus and, before his bodyguard could hope to intervene, her sword blade shot out and with a slash scored his right cheek.

Marcus sat on his horse, rigidly still. He had knowledge and an instinct of what was going to come next.

Jodocca shouted, 'I pronounce a geasa on this man for as long as he shall live!' Then she swung her horse around and joined her companions who had awaited. They all broke into a brisk canter and began to melt from sight.

Crispus watched the blood trickle in a long thin stream down Marcus's face. 'What in Hades was all that about?'

Marcus turned to him a bleak look on his face. 'It is my brand,' he started to explain, then seeing Crispus was totally in the dark he went into more detail. 'A geasa on a person means that no one may harm or kill him except the person who pronounced the geasa. It is one of their customs, and is kept faithfully. Within no time at all it will be all

114

over this island that my carcase belongs to her. I can go into any battle, fight any Briton, and not one weapon will be lifted against me. Indeed I will be treated as if I had leprosy.'

Crispus was stunned into silence from total amazement. Then the full implications hit him and he pulled a face. 'That means your person is safe and is virtually sacred so it makes a total mockery of your remaining both an officer and a soldier!'

'Exactly!' Marcus agreed between clenched teeth. 'She has made me the biggest fool on this island and what can I do about it?— especially when I still love her!'

EIGHT

Crispus finished cleansing the facial wound, then turned to examine the effects of the dead Roman's gear which the maniple leader had brought into him. He kept giving his friend a surreptitious glance. Marcus was busily writing on some fine parchment preparing a report for Scapula. Now and again he would lift his eyes and stare bleakly at the tent's wall. They would almost reverberate with sadness and Crispus gritted his teeth. That female was poison. She had to be. He turned his attention back to the belongings of Marius. After a while he stopped and frowned heavily.What

115

was this? He studied the object in his hand, looked again, went to speak to his officer, then thought better of it as Marcus lifted his head.

'There, that's done, and Scapula can pick the bones out of it. You might as well know. I've made up my mind. I want a very early discharge. I have had enough.'

Crispus thought about the statement for a few seconds, while he sorted out delicate words. 'And what will you do with yourself?'

Marcus gave him a frank look. 'I'm going after that female, and I'm going to make her mine, if it's the last thing I do in my life. I've done my share for Rome and I'm useless as a soldier with her geasa on me. I intend to find where she's gone and what she's doing and then I'll try again.'

Crispus gave a shake of his head almost in desperation. This was not love. It was total obsession. 'Well,' he started dubiously not quite knowing how to frame his thoughts, 'if you are really determined then I'll get out of the Legion as well. I cannot stand by and see you go stamping all over this island, making a fool of yourself over that female without me being around to watch your back. Anyhow, I've given years of my life to Rome, and I must admit the thought of going off free is very attractive.'

Marcus eyed him. Deeply touched. 'What about finances?'

Crispus grinned. 'I've enough on deposit, for whatever I want in my life. Perhaps, after all, I might have to run my eyes over all these British females!'

Marcus bent his head. It would be better to have a companion. 'If you are quite sure I would very much welcome your company but first I have to go back to the fort. It is my duty to give Scapula a verbal as well as written report. I wonder where she is?' he mused.

Crispus snorted. 'They have all vanished into thin air. I sent a runner to Gloucester, but they've not been there, nor have they been on the outskirts,' he started.

Marcus considered. 'I bet I know which way she went then,' he mused thoughtfully. 'After this affair, they would go out of their way to dodge us and I bet they headed towards Cirencester, which is their Dubonnii capital. They know the lie of the land much better than us. Take us away from our roads and we are sitting targets for them with their guerrilla warfare and they certainly excel at that,' he said thoughtfully.

Crispus decided to change the subject. 'I've been going through the dead man's effects. Nothing of value, except this and this!' and he handed two objects to Marcus.

With a frown, Marcus took them and studied both very carefully then he gave his friend a long calculating look. 'Are you thinking what I'm now thinking?' he asked carefully.

Crispus nodded firmly. 'Very much so. What do we do?'

Marcus considered for a minute, then snatched another piece of parchment and started to write, while Crispus leaned over his shoulder curiously. 'Yes!' he said slowly. 'Yes, indeed!'

'When I've finished seeing Scapula I'm going to seal all this, then do another note, and get Sellus to handle that end. I am not interested in going there myself, because I know she's not there,' he explained.

Crispus considered and nodded his head sagely. 'Smart move, and you are not directly involved!'

*   *   *

Sellus was deeply worried. His discharge had come through, and he should have been full of pleasure but all this had been flattened when Marcus Gaius and Crispus rode unexpectedly back to the fort and the officer was closeted a long time with the governor. What it was all about, he did not really know and was not particularly interested.

What he did now know was that he was worried to death. The more he saw of Macha the more smitten he became but she was very hard work indeed. Twice she had boxed his ears for remarks that he considered bright and friendly, but that obviously ruffled her quickly disturbed feathers. Now he was a bit more cautious in what he said to her because she had a very powerful right arm as he had found to his cost on a number of occasions.

He had received an enormous shock when Crispus had bawled at him to go into the officer's tent. Sellus did not care for the breed. It was not that he was hostile to superior rank; more to the point, he was only used to being ignored by them. Marcus Gaius had already helped him by pushing him towards a woman, for which he was grateful even if the courtship was laborious. When he was told to go into the tent, even though now a discharged soldier, he felt instant guilt. What on earth had he done? Such high-ranking officers did not get involved with the likes of him unless there was trouble.

The officer had been astonishingly affable which, if Marcus had but known it, only made Sellus even more agitated with worry. His superior must surely be leading up to something very dramatic and this had indeed proved the case. He had no idea that Crispus had confirmed to Marcus that he was a man with tight lips, and with more commonsense than the run-of-the-mill ranker.

Marcus had explained what he thought it necessary for Sellus to know, then handed over to him a sealed pouch with an extra note. That too was sealed. 'Keep both of these very hidden until you have an opportunity to be alone with the woman Macha. It is of critical importance that no one at all must ever know about this. No one!' Marcus had emphasised. 'When you have done this, and as soon as possible, come and report back to me, what the woman said and make sure I am absolutely alone. I hasten to add, this is nothing detrimental nor treacherous to Rome!'

It was Crispus who had advised him to say this, and Marcus saw the wisdom. 'Well?'

'Yes sir! I can even ride down this afternoon, but—' He paused heavily. 'My courtship is not going at all well. The lady is very strong-minded, and she has a powerful right hand, which I have felt on more than one occasion,' he complained. 'But I'll do what I can and let you know, in private,' he promised.

Marcus understood his precarious position, only too well. Like mother, like daughter. Both from the same strong chip of wood. With tongue slightly in cheek, he added, 'Oh who knows, she might look upon you a little more favourably after this and more I cannot say.'

Sellus rode slowly, and turned the puzzle over in his mind. At the same time, he wondered which was the best way to start his errand. What kind of mood would Macha be in? She was such a dynamic woman because she had certainly gone through that vill like a winter gale. It was vastly different in appearance since he had first seen it. The old latrines, for example, had been covered over with soil and fresh ones dug at a more adequate distance. These he knew were for only so many days, then Macha had the men dig fresh ones.

All the rubbish that had permeated the place had been picked up and now it was really tidy. Huts had been opened to the weather, and everything inside thrown out and burned. New grasses had been cut and were drying out for fresh bedding or floor covering. Hides and cloaks had been washed in the river and hung out to dry. The cattle had been moved into a fresh area with a new stockade fence built to protect them. Even the small children looked fresher and cleaner; certainly the other adults did. It was as if Macha had made them all wash themselves in the river. The sentries were much more alert too, and Macha rotated them more often, so they did not have time to get bored or lax. Also, she had a wicked habit of walking around and appearing when least expected, which kept everyone on their toes. Even their hunting weapons were clean and sharper. What a woman, he marvelled, but just how could he get her to look upon him more favourably? That was the conundrum.

He dismounted after passing an alert century, tied his mount to a fence pole, then

121

strode out among the British homes. All of them were used to him now and he even received a couple of nods of recognition and acceptance. He suspected that the whole vill knew about his attempts to court their chief and that both of them provided quite a good degree of entertainment.

He walked to her home, called out, then entered carefully. He had done this once before, without announcing himself and met a spear at his throat.

Macha sat upon a stool, head bent over a tunic she was mending. She looked up and glowered at him. 'You here again? What is it this time?' she snapped.

Sellus felt his heart sink a little. She was obviously in one of those moods, then he remembered his officer's words but first things first. 'I'm here again because I want to marry you!' he began hopefully. 'You see—!'

'No! *You* see. I think you're mad, quite crazy, and I do not like you, so that's that!'

He held his ground and refused to be abashed. 'Why not?'

That made Macha pause thoughtfully. Deep down she liked him and their sparring was good fun, and she was glad of it. The last few weeks had been terrible. Her father's death and the manner of it had appalled all of them but she was very proud of the way her daughter had handled the whole situation. In a sneaking way, she was not sorry. The Roman officer had been dealt such a crushing blow. She knew her daughter only too well. In Jodocca there was great passion. She could love and hate with equal ferocity, and, when she heard Jodocca had pronounced a geasa upon Marcus Gaius, she had even felt some pity for him. As an outlandish foreigner, invader and trespasser, did he really understand all that a geasa entailed? She doubted this, which made her pity the officer. Poor thing, she mused, he is finished in Britain, and might even end up the laughing stock of Rome but at least that meant he would quit their island in time. There was now no danger of a match between him and Jodocca.

'You irritate me,' she said at last, and looked at Sellus. He certainly wasn't bad looking, because she knew she was no beauty at her age. She suspected he would strip well, and, for a few crazy moments, she wondered how well he would perform in bed. She guessed he would be more than adequate to satisfy her needs, because she was lonely, had been sex starved over the years. She had all the healthy natural appetites, and she had been a widow for far too long. Indeed, some widower Britons had been hanging around her for over a year, but not one attracted her like this insolent Roman.

What really stuck in her throat was the fact that when it had been Jodocca and her Roman officer she had been vitriolic in condemnation, so how could she let herself get involved now? It was downright embarrassing. Yet no matter how often and how cruelly she snubbed him, back he would come again, seemingly unabashed as persistent as flies around a carcase, and even giving her little gifts. She had always returned these, of course; she was far too sharp to be caught that way.

Sellus decided to attack from a fresh angle.

'You are a lousy liar!' Macha bridled with fury. 'How dare you?'

'Easily!' he told her cheerfully. 'Whenever I'm around you, your nipples harden. I can see them through your tunic. I bet if I put my hand between your legs you'd be nice and wet already for me!'

Macha was rendered speechless for once. There was no retort cruel enough that sprang to mind. Besides, more to the point, she knew he was accurate, and this made her blush wildly.

'See! You've gone red!' Sellus chuckled. 'I'm going to have you,' he continued smoothly. 'One way or the other you are going to be mine, so you better get that idea well and truly into your head, and accept it!'

'Sellus!' Macha thundered, then realised it was the first time she had ever used his name. He positively beamed down at her and she stifled an oath. What could she do with him?

Her shoulders sagged a moment wearily. He was impossible to snub, and she knew she respected him for this.

'Enough of that though,' Sellus said, and his tone became serious. He drew up a second stool and sat facing her, his expression grave.

Macha stilled with alarm, as instinct warned her something was coming which she would not like. 'What is it?' She wanted to know automatically lowering her voice. Had something terrible happened to her daughter? Was he now preparing the way for her to learn the worst? Her heart thundered with panic.

'Where is your daughter?' he asked her quietly.

This was the last thing Macha expected. 'Why? What's happened?'

'Nothing has as far as I know,' he replied soothingly, 'but it is important I know her whereabouts.'

Macha drew herself erect. 'I don't know and if I did, I'd not tell a Roman!' she retorted.

Sellus nodded sagely to himself. So far, this was going exactly as the officer had predicted, so he started again. 'It's critically important she be found. There is the most urgent message for her, for her eyes alone too, I must add.'

Now Macha smiled with disbelief. 'From whom?'

'Senior Centurion Marcus Gaius!'

'Him! What's his game now?' Macha grated, eyes narrow with suspicion.

Sellus gave another little nod of confirmation. 'I don't exactly know,' he admitted. 'All I was told there was a message, which must reach your daughter as it was of critical importance to her safety and general welfare,' and slowly he reached into his tunic and removed a small pouch. 'Here! It's in here and what it's about I don't know, nor do I want to know. You can see it's sealed.'

Macha took the pouch and handled it as if it might explode, while her mind worked at lightning speed. As it came from him, it could only be some wild plan of his to win back her affections again. As soon as Sellus had gone she would burn it. Now that Jodocca had made the break with the Roman she would not be a party to anything that might bring them together again.

'I'll take it then,' she said coolly.

Again Sellus marvelled at how the officer had outguessed the woman and her reactions. 'Can you read Latin?' he asked gently.

'Of course I can. Latin and even the Druids' runic writing. We are not all illiterate!'

Sellus dived into another little pocket and produced a short, flimsy parchment, which he passed over. Macha took it doubtfully, then bent her head to read. Its message was succinct and very clear.

In this pouch is something which I consider may endanger your daughter's welfare, and perhaps even her life. I have no idea where she is at present, otherwise I would send it direct with a runner. For both our sakes I think it would be prudent if you saw or arranged for her to have the contents of this pouch as quickly as possible.

MARCUS GAIUS

Macha was completely taken aback and totally baffled. Her fingers prodded unimpressed at the pouch's contents but she ended up none the wiser. His words seem genuine, and she considered this situation, with deep unease. She did not know for sure where Jodocca might be, but she did know in which direction she was heading and for what purpose. She looked over at Sellus with fresh worry.

'What kind of a man is he?' she asked in a low voice.

Sellus gave her a slow smile. 'He is a magnificent, quite outstanding officer and man. He is one of the very few who would take a genuine interest in the lower ranks like myself. He is reliable, sound and honest. I considered myself fortunate to serve under him.'

'From what you say he is not the type to get

into a flap about nothing?' and Macha now wondered yet again if this was another ploy to try and re-establish a relationship with her daughter. She was torn with confusion, but knew she had no alternative than to get the pouch to Jodocca as quickly as possible. She would pick some agile youngster from the vill and get him off very quickly once this constantly intruding Roman had departed. 'Do you swear by all the gods in which you believe that you know nothing about what is in this pouch?'

Sellus pulled himself erect and became very serious. 'I swear by Jupiter!'

Macha sensed he told the truth and also, at the same time, had empathy to realise and understand his difficulty on this specific errand. A bit of mischief twinkled in her eyes. 'Did your officer mention much about me?'

A slow grin slid over his face. 'He did! He wanted to know how my courtship was proceeding. I told him that I thought you were quite wonderful. That you were the woman I have been looking for, for a long time, but that you appear to hate me!' and now Sellus became very serious. 'But win you I will!' and he stood. It was time he went, and it was also a good opportunity to leave her with something about which to think. He paused at the doorway, for one last sentence. 'High-ranking officers don't usually send messages through the likes of me unless they are of critical

128

importance!' and he turned on his heels and left her to mull over the whole situation.

Sellus yearned to take her in his arms, but his wisdom told him to go now and stay right out of her sight for quite a while. Let her stew a bit. It might just bring her to her senses.

* * *

'Silures!' Jodocca grunted. It had been a long ride from near Cirencester, but they had not seen one Roman and had approached the River Severn almost in solitude. They had crossed the river at a narrow point, and it had not been all that unpleasant, although cold. She had taken the opportunity to have a quick swim, wash her hair, get out of her soiled clothes and bundle them into a pack on the horse's back to be dealt with much later. She and Verica had retired behind some bushes and helped each other with their toilet and now both of them glowed with health and well-being.

Now they were entering another tribe's territory, that of the Silures, against whom, so word had reached them, the Governor had issued nothing but an ethnic cleansing order. Just who did that arrogant Scapula think he was? Now they were to enter another's tribal territory, certain rituals and courtesies had to be gone through. The Silures had appeared as if from nowhere, which meant they had a good scout system.

Between the Dubonnii and Silures had been flurries of inter-tribal fighting in the past but nothing vitriolic enough to constitute downright warfare. Sometimes the two had even combined forces against a common foe, so between them lay a degree of respect. There had even been past occasions when tribal marriages had taken place, an excellent way for both tribes to have new blood in their breeding. Their customs were very similar, and each understood the other's dialect. They carried similar weapons, but lived totally different lives.

The Dubonnii were forest dwellers. They were only completely happy when under or near trees, which, not only objects of beauty, were also utilitarian for hiding purposes. The land of the Silures was craggy, peaked and could be highly cruel. Few trees grew on their mountains' sides, so they were a people of the open. When they visited the Dubonnii, they felt smothered by the trees, and very uneasy, while the Dubonnii easily worried at the bleak mountains, narrow passes and thundering, bitterly cold mountain streams.

Secretly, Jodocca considered her people much superior. They were certainly better educated and more knowledgeable about life in general, because they moved with the times. The Silures still had both feet in the past, and it was not always their fault. They were often imprisoned in their mountains during the winter months. Their culture was minimal and their ways were often crude and harsh, but no one could dispute or disparage their aggressive fighting qualities. No tribe could have better allies in war than the Silures.

Deep down, though, Jodocca had a tiny grain of reservation about them. Just how far could they really be trusted when it came down to the nitty-gritty? They were a stiff-necked lot, highly independent, so would they willingly place themselves under a central command? They knew her, of course. Her reputation was known just about everywhere. They also knew what had happened to the two old men, and they approved with great pleasure the clever way in which she had obtained vengeance for every Briton on the island. This had elevated her even more in their eyes.

'Lady Jodocca!' their leader hailed with greeting. 'I'm Llyn of the tuath and vill of Chief Kersun!'

Jodocca knew out of common courtesy she should really make her number with the Silures' chief but this journey had already been then delayed far too long. Caratacus would think she was not coming at all and it was imperative that he knew the Roman strength in her tribal area. She suspected many of those troops would be moved northwards ready for the mother of all battles when the Romans would be finally defeated. 'Are you with us and Caratacus to kill the Romans once and for all?' she asked.

Llyn beamed enthusiastically. 'We all are unto the death!'

Jodocca smiled at this quick response, then wondered how these wild fighters could be persuaded to battle in one group and not go off on individual forays of personal vengeance. They could be a tricky lot to handle at any time, let alone when their bloodlust was up.

'Where is your war band?' she wanted to know next.

Llyn looked like a wild man. His hair was long and thick, coming down to his shoulders. It was also greasy with dirt. Although he wore a tunic and trousers of a dark brown shade, they were all very much the worse for wear. It was obvious he was totally disinterested in his personal appearance. His weapons, though were of good quality, and very workmanlike. When it came down to it, warfare was about weapons and the men who wielded them and not about cleanliness and dress.

'Our war band left a few days ago to liaise with Caratacus. We knew you were coming, of course, and we were left behind to greet you.'

'How many of the enemy are there in this area?'

Llyn laughed and showed dazzling white teeth. 'Very few in our area. When we catch them out foraging or scouting we just kill!' he chortled.

This told Jodocca there were no forts in the area, which meant she could relax a little. The Romans had not really come this way, building their roads instead for the quick transfer of their fighting men from one point to another.

'Do you ride under my command on order?' she asked sternly.

Llyn grinned again. He was fascinated by her as a famous champion fighter, and also the female warrior who had placed a geasa on a high-ranking Roman officer. 'I'll fight under anyone's command, if it gives me the chance to kill Romans!'

'Do you have chariots and, if so, where are they?' Jodocca wanted to know. Their kind of country most certainly did not lend itself to chariots, but most tribes had some tucked away in a good hiding place for mobile guerrilla warfare.

'We shall catch up with them shortly, Lady. They started last, because they can make better time in the kind of terrain we will be entering,' Llyn explained to her.

Jodocca turned and grinned at Verica. 'When we get to the chariots, you will certainly come into your own.' She turned to Cathus: 'You don't know it yet, but your wife is good with horses in a chariot. She can just about make one sit up and beg.'

Cathus was surprised. He had seen British war chariots, and privately thought them useless. They were flimsy objects made from wickerwork, but they did have knife blades attached to their wheels. After the solid Roman efforts, he had been inclined to scorn them, but, upon reflection, he admitted they would have superior speed and excellent manoeuvrability. The knives sticking out of the wheels were very lethal indeed. It all depended upon the type of ground on which a battle would be held. So his wife was a champion at something, and he beamed proudly at her.

'Llyn, how far are we from Caratacus?' Jodocca wanted to know next.

He shrugged, while he calculated. 'Two days or three at the most, if we make a good steady pace.'

Jodocca nodded sagely. She knew perfectly well it took considerable time to gather a large fighting force together. It was not simply a case of getting the fighters into one spot, there were all the logistical arrangements, the most important of which by far were for all the horses.

They camped relatively early and Jodocca was glad to walk around a bit on foot. Her mind still bubbled with recent past events, and her heart see-sawed with violent emotions. She simply could not forget the wonderful week that she had spent with him but neither could she clean from her mind Lud's terrible death. She was mature enough to acknowledge that she was involved in a mixture of love-hate memories. One moment, she told herself hers had been a lucky escape, then the next moment she felt a great yearning to see him again. She almost regretted that geasa, but, deep down, she knew they were both, one day, doomed to fight it out.

'Lady!' Riothamus called sharply, sprinting up to her. 'A courier has arrived, and wishes to see you urgently!'

Jodocca started. She had been so engrossed in her unpleasant thoughts she had failed to hear horses' hooves. 'Bring him here then, right away!'

Her bodyguard returned immediately, and Jodocca's eyes widened with shock and alarm. 'Hoel! What is this? What are you doing here? Is anything wrong at home? How did you find us?'

Hoel was from her vill and was well-known for being totally unable to track a rabbit even two yards from its burrow. He was young and fresh-faced, but would never be a warrior, because he had been born with a withered arm and a permanent limp from one week old, but he was an excellent horseman.

'It took some doing, Lady. I managed to sidle through Gloucester, but gathered you had never gone that way so I worked it out you had taken a long sweep to dodge the Romans and cross the river at a narrow point.'

'Did anyone see you in Gloucester who knew you?' she asked him carefully.

He flashed a grin at her: 'No, Lady, but I saw that bag of fat wobbling around talking to all the Romans who would listen to him!' and he paused before continuing. 'I think some of them are already fed up with his tongue and they are but mocking him.'

Jodocca knew this would be so. Their useless old chief had thought to do well for himself but the Romans were nobody's fools and Vercingetorix would end up the butt of the town. She almost—but not quite—felt sorry for him. He was such a pathetic sight . . . but he did know them all, which meant really none of them could ever take a shortcut through Gloucester in safety.

'There is nothing wrong at home, Lady, but your mother said it was very important that I find you and give you this, and to put it in your hands only,' he said in a little rush of words. He felt embarrassed at being the object of many eyes as he handed over a small pouch with a piece of sealed parchment.

Jodocca took it, frowned, and turned aside. She could feel everyone's eyes on her shoulders as they almost quivered with curiosity. She nodded to Verica to take care of Hoel's welfare, then she walked right away from everyone so she could be totally alone and private.

Jodocca opened the leather pouch, peeped inside, then withdrew a thin parchment letter and something hard also wrapped up.

Daughter, this was delivered to me by the Roman Sellus who thinks he is to marry me. It comes from your Roman officer. Sellus swears he does not know what is inside and I do believe him. I know nothing more. Take care. Love MOTHER

She warily opened the other small packet and found another note that made her frown.

This was .found in the effects of the German murderer. Take particular notice of the small scrawled note. I think it is important for you and I advise reflection and great caution.

MARCUS GAIUS

She then opened the final, stained note, read it, then looked into the distance while her mind worked furiously. She read and re-read the dirty note, then took the other contents into her left hand. How true was this? Was it even possible? Could it be some kind of ploy from—him? She bit her bottom lip, working out complicated permutations. Her instinct told her this was no fancy Roman

137

game, which meant . . . Her eyes went as cold as ice chips. Her face was transformed into a mask of hatred and she walked in between some trees. She must think all of this out very carefully indeed and certainly confide in no one. She must also not let on, by word or deed, what facts were now hers. They must, they simply must get to Caratacus first. Then she would discuss it with him and make her decision. Deep down, she also felt sick at heart. Marcus Gaius would never go to so much trouble for trivialities. He had to be, must be—factually correct.

NINE

Tristus felt utterly miserable. He had never dreamed this island could be so bitingly cold and wet, although he admitted the trouble was that he was wearing the wrong clothes. Besides, he reminded himself firmly, what was physical discomfort to him when he realised what a supreme sacrifice had already been made?

He had walked about for so long, wandering through the town, and that vill. Always when he tried to talk, he had been jeered at and mocked to the extent that his feelings sank to the bottom of his personal pit. They would always climb again with each new dawn, by which time his resolution was firm once more.

Right now, though, he was so tired it was difficult to push one leg before the other. He shivered with cold, and he was so ravenously hungry it would have been incredibly easy to lie down and just give up. He had spotted the small campfire from a distance and wondered uneasily who had made it? It would not be Romans because they were thin on the ground around here, so it had to be Britons. How hostile would they be to him? His nostrils twitched. Was that roast meat he could smell? His mouth filled with saliva, and his empty stomach jabbed painfully. Was there a chance of a morsel of food?

Two men jumped on him from either side, and he was flung to the ground while his hands were roughly tied. Then he was hauled to his feet and dragged forward unceremoniously towards the fire's light.

'Lady! We have an intruder!'

Jodocca stifled a groan. Now what? As if she hadn't enough on her mind and in her aching heart. She stood up wearily as the prisoner was dragged before her.

Well, she thought, what kind of scarecrow is this? The man was tall and cadaverously thin. His hair was long and dark, but some attempt had been made to keep it clean, and it was held at the nape of the neck with a piece of cord. His eyebrows were as black as night and

139

his face displayed weather-beaten skin, where it had been exposed to the elements. He was dressed in a long flowing robe, but she could not be sure whether this was brown or dirty. The man did not grovel and, strangely, neither did he show fear.

'Who are you and what do you want?' she asked stiffly.

The man looked at her and threw an eloquent shrug. For a long time now, Tristus had been trying to learn the outlandish British language, involving so many tribes, but he found it very difficult.

Jodocca understood and switched to her polished, highly educated Latin. The man's eyes opened wide with surprise. He tilted his head slightly as if he had to adjust his sight, then looked down at her. A slow smile played over a face which was not unhandsome, but which bore deep pain lines from some awful experiences. He looked down at his right foot, which seemed to move as if of its own accord.

Jodocca sensed she was supposed to gaze in that direction and did so. Very carefully, almost elegantly, the man's booted toe outlined a fish. Then he halted, stood straight again, and looked her firmly in her vivid blue eyes.

She was taken aback, then Lud's words carne tumbling down memory lane. A fish! What did that mean? What was it Lud had said about something new coming? She saw that his eyes held an inquisitive glow.

'My name is Tristus, and I come from Gaul,' he replied in gentle and beautiful Latin.

Jodocca was suspicious. 'What are you doing here then? You are a long way from the Continent.'

'To talk to those who will listen!' was his enigmatic reply.

It all flooded back to her, and she had a flashing instinct that his peculiar reply was very much like one Lud would have given her. Just another riddle!

'Talk about what?' she barked impatiently. She felt utterly exhausted; with her horrendous mental problems it was almost too difficult to think straight, let alone play guessing games. It occurred to her that his deep brown eyes were now weighing her up! 'What exactly do you want here and now?'

'Refuge, Lady, and a little food, please.'

Jodocca blinked and eyed him again even more carefully. He was thin enough to blow over in a puff of wind, and then she heard the dull rumble of a very empty stomach, and she made up her mind.

'Eat with us,' she offered, 'but if you have not eaten for a while go very slowly or you will be horribly sick. It is boar and such meat is rich.' She turned to her interested spectators. 'Let him stay for a bit. Arms?'

The sentries shook their heads. 'Only his

eating dagger, Lady!'

They crowded around him, curious, highly inquisitive and sensing some new story. Like all the tribes of Britain, they loved nothing better than a story before the evening campfire.

Jodocca sat between two of Llyn's men. This strange man did not look capable of attacking a fly but again her superb leadership traits showed when she placed him in a position where he could do the least harm if he should be perfidious.

Tristus ate very slowly, with delicate manners, savouring each carefully chewed mouthful before allowing it to slide down to an eagerly awaiting stomach. He showed up the uncouth Silures and he even made Jodocca pull herself together. When he had taken his fill and refreshed himself with the mead that they carried, she invited him to sit next to her.

He revelled in losing the griping stomach pains, and the food was delicious after so long eating simple herbs and insects. He threw a look around, noting just one other female and a small gang of men who looked like nothing but a gang of thugs. He had not missed how they all deferred to her, and he too, when he first crossed to Britain, had made it his business to learn something of tribal culture. He knew now he was expected to pay for his meal in the one way these people would appreciate. Tell them a story, and this he was more than ready to do. After all, what better story was there than that of the Christ?

Jodocca opened the conversation ball first. 'Refuge from whom?'

'Romans!' he replied in a low voice. 'The chance to make a new life away from them once and for all. A chance to tell the Story. A chance perhaps to join with others. We are very few in number at the moment, but our movement will grow as we share our Belief. Many have died in Rome. Some have been killed in the games—thrown against the wild beasts. Some have been crucified as He was. For the time being though, we have to be careful and prudent.'

Jodocca mulled over these words after translating for those whose Latin was non-existent. She was still rather puzzled. 'Why should you and your companions be killed? Do you attack Romans?'

'We are killed because we Believe!'

'In what though?'

He studied her and could sense impatience, scepticism, fatigue, grief—and something else, which was hard and cruel. She carried her leadership lightly, but it was obvious she had a spine of steel. She had to be good to control this gang of thugs, because control them she certainly did. The young woman had suffered, but he sensed she had to go through more fire yet. With his rare gift of prescience, his heart went out to her.

'It is a long story,' he began gently. 'Perhaps it should be told when everyone is fresh,' he hinted delicately. Now his stomach was satisfied his own eyes felt very heavy but as a guest he could hardly go to sleep now.

Jodocca was incredibly sharp. She read through him and concurred. 'It will keep for another day, when we are all fresher. Our guest is tired, and I have a lot of deep thinking to do.' That was accurate, she told herself. So much thinking! Her mind swivelled in many directions yet she knew she must be fresher on another day to view from a fresh perspective.

'Ride with us for a while. We have some spare horses, and then you can tell us your story another evening,' she invited. This man would do them no harm. He was of far too gentle a nature and the fact he was against Romans was a good enough passport for all of them.

To her astonishment, she slept very well, only awakening just prior to the dawn, settled upon her resolve and knowing what she had to do in the very near future. She had no intention of hurrying, because the fit had to be perfect.

They broke their fast early and quickly mounted up after seeing the young Hoel back on his journey with a strict warning from Jodocca to avoid Gloucester and bumping into Vercingetorix.

Jodocca rode with the thin man, and invited him to talk of his life. Storytelling was for the evening campfire. Tristus found it harrowing. He and his wife and child had believed in the Christ but one day he had returned from trading and found them gone. They had been taken as Christians and thrown to the lions. For him it had been the end of the world, and he wished he could have been at home with them to have accompanied them. It was friends who persuaded him to escape from Rome and slowly he had made his way to Gaul, and from there to Britain.

His words were deliberately simple. Not because he thought she would not understand; he had already discovered her high intelligence, but because the story sounded better when told in simple words. He found after this, he had slipped easily into the Christ story, which would of course have to be repeated that evening.

Jodocca listened in total silence. This had to be what her grandfather had meant. How had he known that he and his kind were on their way out to be replaced by followers of a man and a story, which sounded totally outlandish, even ridiculous? That a man had died in a hot land through crucifixion was easy enough to understand, because it was a typical way for Romans to kill.

'So why didn't he and his followers fight back?'

Tristus always found such pacifism virtually impossible for tribes to understand when they revelled so in internecine warfare.

'It was not his way,' and Tristus realised how tame these words must sound.

Riothamus had ridden closely behind them, ears flapping, missing nothing and deeply perturbed. This lady was not herself. Something had happened, because she had become coldly aloof and, flog his wits as he might, he could not think of an explanation. Hoel had brought some kind of message that so disturbed her that she did not even see him now and this rankled. Now there was this stranger with this totally ridiculous story—when would he ever have a chance to have a private talk with her? He would like this before they reached Caratacus, because he had decided it was high time he spoke his mind firmly and laid his suit before her. If he didn't speak out she would never know!

'What do you gain from telling such a story of this Christ?' she demanded to know.

He looked straight into her eyes and chided her very gently. 'Must there always be gain?'

Jodocca knew she had gone red, and she knew now the man was another Lud. He was so wise, he had travelled so far and seen so much, had undergone such personal agony. Yet there was no angry bitterness in him. Once it became known he was a storyteller, he would be in great demand, though people

146

would tease him for his pacifist thoughts. She thought of the fish symbol again. What exactly had Lud known which he had withheld from her, and why had he failed to forecast what would happen concerning Marcus Gaius? She gave an impatient little shake to her head and knew instinctively that this Tristus was every bit as deep as Lud had been. It was time to change the subject.

'What can you do? Is there anything special you know?'

Tristus replied slowly. 'I understand spices and herbs and have some little knowledge of healing,' he explained.

Jodocca brightened, because these were very valuable talents for warriors getting ready for warfare. 'That's splendid!' she told him. 'We might just need your services in the very near future.' Then she decided to give him a little test. 'How do you treat the disease which can affect many of us after a long winter?'

It was a simple question. 'You mean the sickness which makes the gums turn red, the teeth loosen and the whole mouth smell. That is easy. Just eat plenty of green foods from the autumn onwards even if they are only leaves. The first buds of spring are very important and should be eaten raw. Not cooked. I don't know how exactly this helps, but it does!'

'How can I get rid of chilblains?'

'The best thing is to boil and mash root vegetables, make a poultice, cover the chilblains and they will soon go!'

She knew she liked this man. He was simple, direct and honest. He would harm no one and might even prove a valuable asset. He would certainly be in great demand, with his storytelling, though she knew perfectly well this crucified Christ would be mocked for not fighting back as any Briton would.

'You may ride with me unless I am busy with someone else,' she told him, knowing perfectly well she had now started to play a double game.

Tristus was delighted. He had found a refuge at last. If he had a single reservation it was a wish that the climate was a little warmer. He was perfectly aware that the guard who rode directly behind both of them did not like this one little bit. This man was consumed with some kind of bitter jealousy, and he might be all the more dangerous for it.

In was mid-afternoon when they began meeting people, and scouts rolled out to identify them. They trotted the last distance to what was slowly turning into a huge gathering and Jodocca soon spotted her cousin.

'Caratacus!' she cried joyfully; she had not seen him for quite a long period but as long as she could remember there had always been a good feeling between them. Their liking was such that they could immediately take up a conversation from where they last left off.

'Jodocca! At last!' he cried enthusiastically,

striding over to her as she dismounted and grabbing her in a bear hug of delight. He was not a huge warrior, but he was tactician, strategist and soldier, all rolled into one. The shoulders were square, wide and powerful. His arms, bare from the shoulders, had long, lithe muscles that rarely tired. He wore a slight facial beard, light brown in colour, which matched his thick, slightly curly hair. His eyes were grey, which changed with the light, ranging from a misty shade to a deeper stone colour. Now they glowed with delight.

'I heard about Lud,' he said soberly. 'That was a shocking business, but you handled it very well. Where is your geasa-laden Roman now? Dodging you?'

Jodocca pulled a moué. 'I have a lot to discuss with you, cousin. Quite a lot of it bad as well. Can we go somewhere private?'

He eyed her grim countenance as she slipped her arm into his, and led her to his tent. He felt deep unease suddenly assail him. She had changed, and not in a subtle manner. There had to be something very wrong indeed.

'There's a stream in that direction which the females are using, and you'll soon be provided with washing herbs and after that we can have a council meeting,' he told her.

Jodocca shook her head. 'That can all wait. My report first of all!' she began, as they entered his tent. She sat on a stool and took a mug of refreshing mead. 'There's been quite a lot of activity in our land, with the Romans at the fort and that odious Scapula. The Romans are also in strength in other districts, and it is pretty obvious they are going to march against us here. You are their target!'

'I'm more up to date than you. They are already on their march, heading towards us, but not hurrying over much, which is strange.' He mused for a little while. 'Also two Romans are riding quite separately in the same direction? They could be pure observers with a brief to report back to the governor in due course but they are holding themselves aloof from their own kind, even to the extent of cold camping by themselves. I don't like it when Romans take it into their heads to act out of character.'

Jodocca frowned at this latter information, then a thought niggled at her. Two men? Surely not? She would have to think about this later on and see if it was possible to get a detailed description. Now there was another matter to discuss.

'Queen Cartimandua is turning into a real troublemaker.'

Again Jodocca was puzzled. This was the Brigantia tribe and like many others she held this queen in considerable contempt. She had opted for her tribe to be clients of Rome. What had happened to her British spirit?

'Talk has reached me that not all her tribe agree with her. There have been rumblings from numerous directions, and she's even had to contend with a minor civil war. She won, of course. She is too firmly astride the horse to be bucked off so easily, and they are a quarrelsome lot at the best of times. We have some of them here and they seemed to delight in making rows. I have had to lean on them to keep order,' he grumbled.

Jodocca stored this information away for later mental dissection. She knew now was the time to bring up the great problem but Caratacus was in full spate.

'So far we have you Dubonnii, the Silures, some Brigantes and Ordovices, plus a few Druids, so we shall be able to smash the Romans once and for all and start a massive push to get them off our island. The land around here will be good for our chariots and we have excellent lines of communication. Incidentally, did you know that the Romans have plans for a line of forts down your way but on the other side of the river?'

This was news to her and she supposed it made logical sense to a Roman mind. 'That explains something about which I have heard. They have a good detachment of their Pioneer Corps. I suppose these men are for this fort building, and it will be the usual every ten miles. Well, the Romans might have a big shock coming to them yet but, Caratacus, I must speak to you now, on a very grave matter.'

She opened her tunic and removed the pouch from inside a pocket. She opened it and passed the contents to her cousin. He looked at it with a frown, then started to read what was inside as well as examine the heavier contents.

She then began to speak, and as she did so, her eyes became hard, her expression bleak. There was even a small tremble in her hands, as her passion was roused.

Her cousin sat shocked and appalled. It did not seem possible, yet hunt as he might he could find no flaw in her astute deduction. He studied the pouch's contents yet again, and his jaw hardened.

'How do you want to handle this?' He grated with anger only just under control.

Jodocca told him. She had thought about this for hours now. Even when talking to someone else or riding it had been constantly at the back of her mind. She had gone over it again, and again, relentlessly hunting for some other reason, but always she came back to her original deduction.

'So be it!' he told her firmly as she stood. For a few seconds, her shoulders slumped, and one of his hands rested on the left shoulder to squeeze reassuringly. 'You have had much to cope with, though this is a bad business. A very bad business! More than that it is hateful, and I never thought—!'

'Neither did I!'

TEN

'My!' Crispus said. 'You are in a mood today!' but he knew why and was tolerant.

Lucius Crassus had started off this latest trouble. When he heard of Marcus's situation with the British he had nearly fallen about laughing. 'Well,' he had chortled. 'Bested by an enemy female! More fool you but never mind! From what you say about her being a fighter, I'll take her out at the very start so you won't have to worry!'

Marcus had turned red with fury and stepped forward, fists bunched, ready to smash the other in the face. Crispus had been forced to move very quickly indeed to restrain him. The very thought of two officers having a brawl in the fort which housed the bad-tempered Scapula had nearly made his hair stand on end with horror. The retribution would be too horrific to contemplate. He had managed to drag a boiling Marcus away so was it any wonder he was in such a foul temper?

Crispus had his own opinion of Lucius Crassus. He was a typical product of a very wealthy Roman family, who fancied himself as a soldier. It would be very interesting to witness his conduct when up against a mass of howling savages. Talk was so cheap; deeds carried a higher price and he had a sneaking suspicion that, when push did come to a shove, Lucius Crassus might well wish himself back in Rome. It was an indisputable fact that the British were very good fighters indeed, even if wild and undisciplined in his estimation.

Very gradually Marcus came out of his bad temper and eyed his companion. 'Many thanks,' he said feelingly. 'I very nearly made a fool of myself, but I will certainly bear in mind what that rich prig said!'

Crispus knew when to change the subject. 'I take it we cold camp at night by ourselves and have nothing to do with troop movements?'

Marcus nodded, then threw his companion a wan smile. 'I know exactly what you're thinking. All right, so I am an official observer of the battle to come, and I admit that is only half of it. It is her! If I'm being a fool, say so, but I just can't help myself!'

'Yes, you are being a fool! And that's all I'll say about it,' Crispus grated. 'By all the gods, if you do manage to win her, geasa or no geasa, I just hope she proves worth it. Now hadn't we better increase our riding speed? Moving at this pace, the battle is going to end up ancient history!' he said sarcastically.

Marcus muttered a curse, added a grin of agreement and pushed his mount into a loping canter.

*　　*　　*

Macha was sick to the pit of her stomach and there was nothing she could do about it; no one in whom she could confide. The hastily scribbled note from her daughter, carried by Hoel, was written in runic script as well as in a private code developed long ago in the family. It had been an idea suggested by Jodocca's father when alive, and was one neither of them had ever forgotten. It was a fallback for safety and this note was the first Macha had ever received. It had taken her a little while to decipher the signs but when she had read the contents she had been horrified. So much so, that it had crossed her mind to wonder whether Jodocca had not made some hideous miscalculation.

She was deeply miserable with it all and itched to do something, yet she knew she was absolutely powerless.

She did not hear him call out, and the next thing was that Sellus stood before her, his stance more than a little wary. He was never certain how he was going to be received. It could be with angry words, or even a spear thrust if a hunting weapon was handy. Now this woman whom he really fancied, sat in misery, and as she lifted her head, her eyes brimmed with tears.

Sellus was quite shocked at this. 'What is it?

155

Are you unwell?'

Then Macha burst into a flood of weeping, and without hesitation, he strode forward, pulled her to her feet and hugged her. He stroked her hair and marvelled as she laid her head against his chest. He swelled with pride. Something dreadful must have happened for her to turn to him like this.

'Can't you tell me? Is it your daughter?' he asked, very gently.

Macha shook her head miserably, then lifted red-rimmed eyes to study him. 'I can't tell you but it is too awful for words. Jodocca is all right. It is something else,' she gabbled, still a little hysterical.

Sellus frowned, and set his own mind to work remorselessly. It had to be something quite catastrophic to reduce this strong woman to such a state where she turned on him and wanted his comfort. Under other circumstances he would have been delighted. He was deeply puzzled, but slowly started to work it out that it was something to do with the coming battle. Was she so afraid for her daughter's safety? Then he dismissed that idea. He now knew her daughter was a Jodoccus or champion fighter and had taken the female version of the word instead of her normal name of Beltane.

Like all ordinary soldiers, he was familiar with all the low-down gossip, and he knew about Marcus Gaius and this peculiar geasa placed upon him by her daughter. This information had caused considerable amusement among the rank and file and some wit had even dared to suggest that was why the officer had resigned. It was a very dangerous jibe to make and Sellus had refused to pass comment or get involved in any way. He had his own opinion of Marcus Gaius and would definitely not like him as an enemy.

'I'm so sorry,' he placated. 'I think you now know that if there is anything I can do to help you in any way I will!' he vowed firmly.

Macha had regained control of herself, although she continued to sniff. It dawned upon her he was a good man. He could not help being a Roman, and now that he was a civilian she realised she could regard him differently. Had she been too rough and standoffish? 'I cannot tell you a thing but I can tell you this. Give me a little more time!' and she looked him straight in the eyes with the suggestion of a promise.

Sellus's heart swelled with joy. He had great patience and was prepared to wait a while as long as he had her in the end. Whatever it was that had caused her so much distress had been providential for him.

*　　*　　*

The people collected slowly, for the council meeting, although these were not usually held so soon after dawn. Instead of Caratacus, facing them it was Jodocca of the Dubonnii tribe, who was ready to hold centre stage with her bodyguard Riothamus nearby and the adopted Roman on the other. Both men looked at each other, and it was easy to see there was no love lost there.

The storyteller stood to one side, at the rear, where he could watch with interest and also keep out the way. Cathus and Verica stood together, both rather puzzled although for different reasons. Cathus had made remarkable strides in learning the language but he realised he still had a lot to learn about British customs in general. Verica was uncertain what could be going to happen next—council meetings were usually held well into the morning. Then Jodocca stepped forward and held out one hand, to still the general chatter and hold attention.

'People, I ask you to listen to me, please!' and she threw one more swift, assessing look around before continuing. Now she certainly had everyone's attention. 'I have a story to tell you, but it is not a nice one. Many weeks ago, I made a fool of myself,' she started bravely. Caratacus had warned her, only the whole truth would suffice. It would also be a catharsis.

'I fell for a Roman officer on my last trading trip, having met him purely by chance. I was almost besotted with him. I say this to my shame. I also lack the brains of a two year old. There was no sex, but that was more by luck than chance. He wanted me to marry him, to abandon our good way of life and become a Roman matron. Me!'

This produced a ripple of amusement, and even one or two earthy comments were thrown at her. She allowed a little smile to pucker her lips before continuing.

'I hesitated, and I think now it was a warning instinct, but our short friendship had become known, and I simply had no idea of this. We naturally parted, I went on tribal business and the Roman went on his. We were both astounded to be able to meet again, near our local fort, where the governor is stationed at present. It was a difficult, heartrending meeting and we reached a compromise decision to meet up again this coming winter.'

She paused for effect. 'And now we come to the nasty bit. My grandfather, Druid Lud and his companion Osa were both killed in a bestial manner. Roman boot marks were everywhere, and many of you will know the outcome of this event. I challenged the officer to produce the killer and my champion dealt with him. What you do not know, though, is that it was a put-up job from start to finish!'

The people burst into talk, heads turning, and she let them go on for a bit before silencing them with an upraised right hand.

'Unknown to me there was another who

fancied me. He had worked it out about the Roman officer and decided the best way to end that relationship was to have me turn against and hate the Roman—to leave the field clear for him. He arranged for those two old men to be butchered. He passed over quite a number of coins of high-value denarii to pay for the job, and by bad luck or design he picked one of the cruellest men in the XX. An auxiliary to whom killing was obviously fun. A sadist! How did he arrange this? Simplicity itself! He was out one time, saw the Roman foraging party, asked for a temporary truce for a wounded man—who did not exist—then made the arrangements and handed over the money.'

Jodocca paused again, and the people started to murmur, which gradually began to change to a growl.

'How do I know this? It was the Roman officer who told me! Someone went through the dead auxiliary's effects, and there was far more money present than he could possibly have earned. Also, there was a note. This!' And with a dramatic flourish, she produced the pouch and extracted the dirty document.

'This is being kept with Prince Caratacus, but is available for anyone to study. But for now you must just take my word for it. You will see to one side of this writing, rather bad Latin, I might add, there is a detailed map of the secret tracks used by Druids. If our wise old men had not been killed where they were it would simply have been further along.'

An angry murmur rumbled through the crowd, but she waited for silence once more. 'I am almost sorry that I invoked the geasa on the Roman Marcus Gaius because he must have gone to considerable trouble to get this information to me, with this pouch and a warning to be on my guard. However, the geasa stands and one day we will fight. It is the here and now I'm interested in. I want vengeance!'

The crowd roared their approval and agreement. Weapons were clattered against shields to make a thundering, drumming sound and voices bellowed rage. Jodocca spun around and faced Riothamus. 'I never thought you could be so treacherous!' she spat.

The face of Riothamus had turned ugly and red. He then felt a spear jab into the small of his back as he was pushed forward centre stage. He looked around, sweat beading his forehead, while Jodocca squared up to him disgust emanating from every pore in her body.

'Why?' She cried. 'Why have those two old men killed? Did you think I would ever be yours? You are insane!'

Riothamus did not bother to reply, but his keen eyes darted everywhere seeking a loophole through which to escape. He knew what had to come next. He had gambled and lost. It had never entered his head Marius would keep his carefully drawn plan. Why had he done this? Then it dawned on him. Marius had intended to use the plan and his information for the purposes of blackmail, and he, Riothamus, would have been powerless. He cursed himself. The plan had seemed so good. Now it also hit him she had never cared one iota for him. This too had never entered his conceited mind. If he could not have her, then no one else would. He sprang forward, knife drawn in a flash and slashed toward her throat.

His move had been so swift, they were nearly all taken aback. Cathus was not. A deep gut instinct had began to swell with every word the lady had uttered. He had found himself watching Riothamus very carefully indeed. He leapt forward, in one giant bound, and one enormous fist came around and smashed into the man's neck. Riothamus fell as if pole-axed. Cathus snatched up the dropped dagger, ready to kill him.

'No!' Jodocca screeched at him. 'Not that way! We have our customs!'

Verica added her voice. 'You mustn't, Cathus! Just restrain him!'

Jodocca turned to her cousin who stood with an ashen face. Jodocca herself felt very shaken. That had been close. Too close. Perhaps she was not as clever as she had thought.

Men had now lashed the guard's arms behind his back. They heaved him to his feet, and he stood cursing foully, wild-eyed, saliva trickling from his mouth. 'I should have done for you as well, Roman!' he snarled as they took him away to be imprisoned until later.

Jodocca turned to Cathus and gave him a watery smile. 'You saved my life. I owe you,' she said bluntly. 'I now need a new personal bodyguard and would be honoured if you would take the position?'

Cathus flushed with pleasure. 'The honour will be mine, Lady,' he replied and ducked his head in a polite little bow.

Verica hauled him aside beaming from ear to ear. That had all been a little too close for comfort.

'What happens now? An execution?'

Verica hastened to enlighten him. 'Oh no! Jodocca will fight and kill him!'

Cathus gasped with shock. 'What!' he cried. 'That's crazy! A girl can't fight a man! If I'm her new bodyguard . . . that's my job. Man-to-man!'

Verica looked at him with some pity and gave a tiny shake of her. Dear Cathus. He still had so much to learn, and he tried so hard. 'Our Lady has to fight him. No one else can. She is the wronged party. It was her flesh and blood that was murdered, not yours. Furthermore, she is a champion and if she ducked such a fight her name would be ruined for all time.'

'I have never heard anything so idiotic in all my life!'

Verica gave him a smile. 'Do not underestimate anyone, any fighter, just because they are of the opposite sex. You'll see!' she said confidently.

Cathus was quietly appalled and wondered whom he could use as an ally? It was no good going to her cousin. He would be just as bad. He cast an appealing look at the storyteller who had just wandered nearby. He opened his mouth ready to start an argument with anybody, then from his eye corner saw that his wife would be very much against this. He snapped his mouth shut and decided he would have to do something when the time came.

Verica had learned to read his moves and thoughts, because she had developed a great love for this unusual man. She touched his arm reassuringly. 'Don't get worked up about what you cannot change. I wouldn't like to be in the boots of Riothamus later on and he knows this too! Why do you think he tried to take her out by surprise?'

Cathus knew when he was beaten. 'I think you Britons are all mad!'

Verica had to laugh at this. 'Don't forget that includes you now!'

Jodocca strolled past, then halted as she looked at their faces. Verica's twinkled with amusement while Cathus had almost a sulk on his face.

'Hello! What's this? You two been having a row?' she asked with some amusement.

Verica could not help but chuckle at the expression on the face of Cathus. 'Just a slight difference of cultural opinion!' she explained. 'Cathus does not like the idea of you fighting with lethal intent. He says that it's his job now.'

Jodocca turned to him and recognised a mulish obstinacy in her bodyguard's eyes. He opened his mouth to speak his mind, but she forestalled him. 'No! No one can do this but me, and it is expected of me as well. Don't look so put out! I am fully competent, and you might just have a surprise!'

Cathus was left flat-footed, as she turned and walked towards her cousin, then saw Tristus, changed her mind and went to him instead. 'Talk to me!' she hissed.

He was sharp and astute. 'Of course, my daughter,' he began, and, arm in arm, she allowed him to take her where they could be a bit more private. Tristus had missed exactly nothing. He was not exactly delighted at what was obviously to come but he had the discretion to approach from an indirect angle.

'You are quite sure?'

Jodocca smiled up at him, and nodded. 'Very!'

He took a deep breath. He too found some of these British customs quite outlandish, but

165

he knew that women could be as brave as men and, under certain circumstances, far more dangerous with it.

'I take it you are skilled and fast?' he wanted to know next.

Jodocca grinned at him. 'Both!' she reassured. 'I had the best teacher when young. My late father. Because he did not have a son he treated me as one and gave me personal tuition, coached me and made me exactly who I am!'

'I abhor treachery!'Tristus told her as they walked on. People kept out of their way exercising great diplomacy. It had already spread throughout the gathering that this unusual man was like a Druid but that he came with fresh ideas and stories even if they were weird ones. 'And there is none worse than that over sex. Have you dismissed this Roman officer from your mind completely?'

Jodocca knew she had to be scrupulously honest with him because, like her dear old grandfather, he appeared to have the ability to read her mind completely. 'I have tried to and as you will know I am one day fated to fight him, but—' and her words tailed away unhappily. 'It was simply something just not meant to be.'

He halted, turned and faced her, his expression grave. 'Be very careful,' he said gently. 'You still have to face many trials and tribulations on a very hard road before you find peace. It will come, but possibly at a cost,' and he squeezed her right arm with reassurance.

Jodocca gave a tiny shake to her head. 'You and my grandfather would have made a good pair—talking in riddles all the time! I am glad you are with us. Now I must go and prepare,' she told him and turned away to walk briskly back to her cousin's tent. On the way she passed the small stockade, heavily guarded, which held the prisoner.

Riothamus watched her walk past, ignoring him. He writhed with humiliation. If only he could get out, grab a horse and bolt he would, even though he knew he would be an outcast, damned by all. Trapped here, he knew he was going to die one way or the other. He watched her retreating back uneasily. Female she might be, lacking his superior strength and muscle power, but she would be very difficult to tackle. Even if he did manage to beat her there would then be the guards and the rest of the people. Where had it all gone wrong? He had carried a torch for her long before she became a young widow. Perhaps he should have spoken as soon as she was free and single. Instead, he had been over-awed by her rank and position. It was the sight of the golden torque that had always made him hesitate. He cursed. That he should have picked the cruellest man in the XXth was extremely bad luck. Any greedy auxiliary

167

would have done. He was furious with himself and the basic mistakes he had made by acting too impetuously instead of thinking things through more deeply.

It was with relief that he watched the escort approach. They pulled him out, none too gently, into the centre of a large gathering of the people. They allowed him to stretch and flex his muscles, then Caratacus took over.

'You have a short sword and a dagger with a small shield. Go and pick them up and fight when I say, not before. If you attempt to start sooner these men have been ordered to spear you!' and he nodded at three guards nearby who regarded him with total contempt.

Jodocca was similarly armed and waited quite coolly, then advanced to the centre as he came to her. She wondered if he would make the mistake of charging like a bull but his approach was wary.

Jodocca knew Riothamus was an experienced fighter and battle tested. She held herself easily and with confidence, wearing a mocking look on her face. Riothamus was disconcerted at this. He felt the blood suddenly hammer in his temples, and he struck out savagely. To his astonishment his target had vanished. He blinked and felt a sharp stab, in his right side and, looking down, saw blood and he blinked. From where had she come? Then to his chagrin, he felt another stab in the same spot on the opposite side. By all the gods, he had not realised she was so fast with such incredible reflexes.

Jodocca felt satisfied now that she had blood on him, and she waited, eyeing him cagily, almost sure of his next move. He sprang and their blades met with a clang. She had already gripped the hilt firmly but, even so, shock jarred her arm muscles. In her turn she was amazed at the strength and power in his right arm. It would be unwise to allow him to get so near again.

She jumped back, and to one side, and then started stabbing, darting around his shield, little sword pecks while, at the same time, she manipulated her shield so it took all of his blows. She was everywhere and nowhere, her figure a blur of action, her sword blade twinkling in the sun.

Riothamus started to lose his temper. She was making a fool of him, disdaining to stand and fight, blade to blade, with power and strength alone. Her rapid, lightning thrusts were awesome and frightening, and he found he had to keep changing his stance and unbalancing himself but still her sword tip kept biting. Not one wound was fatal but they were all weakening and now he bled freely.

He lunged, trying to catch her unawares but she caught the blow on her shield and deflected its power, then suddenly her sword bit again. This time it rested longer and went in much deeper. He knew a muscle had been

169

cut in his flank and immediately winced, his weight favouring it. This was bad, because now he was lopsided.

Jodocca felt herself start to sweat slightly and decided this was going on long enough. She had played with him, made him pay a little for Lud and Osa but now it was crunch time. She stood, feet slightly apart, and mocked him to come forward.

He did. At last Riothamus thought, 'Now I have a target in one place,' and his blade sang through the air but though she did not move her shield did. It was a very good shield, but, even so, a split started to show and he grinned maliciously. He lifted his great right arm for the final blow when, to his disbelieving horror, something slid under his arm.

Her sword travelled fast and hard. It entered between two ribs and continued moving on as Jodocca followed it with her body weight, driving it home almost to the hilt.

Riothamus stood there, dead on his feet, his heart ruptured; then, with a neat twist, a savage jerk, Jodocca released her blade, extracted it, then hastily jumped back as the dead body crashed to the ground. It half rolled once and lay still while blood pooled underneath.

Jodocca stared down at him impassively. Her mind swirled with emotion as she could now accept the two old men's deaths. With enormous dignity, she bent and wiped her blade on some of the grass still untrammelled. She sheathed her sword and turned to a proud cousin, an absolutely stunned bodyguard and a very relieved storyteller. The spectators roared their approval and came crowding around her, slapping her on the back, offering her drink, celebrating with her, already talking about each blow and parry.

Cathus had never been so thunderstruck in all his life. She was better than him! What a fantastic speed! What incredible reflexes! He blinked, gave a tiny shake of bemusement to his head, and knew what was expected of him next. He bulled his way through the excited throng until he was able to face her. 'Your orders, Lady?' he asked as he held his Roman javelin in sincere salute.

Jodocca blinked. 'Orders?' and she looked around at the excited faces and heard the shouts of her enthusiastic supporters. 'We prepare for Romans!' She paused a little theatrically and raised her voice in a shout. 'We prepare to defend our land against these upstarts, once and for all!'

With that, the gathering erupted into bellows of confidence and they began to race around, punching and slapping each other like wild children.

Cathus watched this with growing unease. He could understand their need to celebrate right now, but it suddenly hit him that he who been used to the rigid and almost unassailable discipline of a fighting Legion, might be getting a foretaste of what these wild people would be like in battle. A great stone sank to the bottom of his stomach.

ELEVEN

Marcus and Crispus sat their horses side by side. They were at the top of a steep hill from which they had excellent visibility all around. The Romans had made their night camp early and both men examined it critically. So far, Lucius Crassus did not appear to have put a foot wrong. The camp was the usual utilitarian Roman effort and it bristled with efficiency.

'So far so good,' Marcus said slowly, 'but I think he's keeping the auxiliary cavalry too far to the rear.'

Crispus was inclined to agree. 'Unless it's a ploy,' he suggested. 'I doubt the British know they are there. He could unleash them to mop up,' he mused slowly and Marcus nodded reluctantly. *He* should be down there leading those men. Not stuck up here like grand spectators at the Games. He wondered where *she* was. They had spied on the enormous horde of the Britons who had camped in the other direction in their usual rabble of activity. Such close proximity when they were only two in number was not without its own hazards. They could soon be picked off by wandering Britons so they were ultra-secretive and took it in turns at night to keep a watch. They lived on the dried foods they carried and drank plain water. They were armed to their teeth and their horses were the best possible. Both knew in a back-to-back action against reasonable numbers, they could give an excellent account of themselves. But secrecy was the order of the day.

The two eyed the ground carefully. It was not exactly a valley as such, but there were good flat stretches to right and left while the centre portion was strewn with pebbles, and some large stones.

'Those flat stretches will be dangerous, if they have many of their chariots with knives at the wheels,' he commented thoughtfully. 'I know what I would do in that case. March the men over the rough ground, where they are safe from chariot attack, but are capable of throwing javelins and pilums to take out the chariot drivers.'

Crispus nodded sagely. This would be standard warfare procedure under the current circumstances, and the wave of missiles thrown with their great accuracy would devastate any enemy, and certainly halt an advance.

'It's going to be a walkover,' Marcus added heavily. 'There's not a chance the British can win.'

*   *   *

Cathus was totally horrified, unable to believe his eyes or his ears. He stared around with sinking heart and closed his eyes momentarily. Was this some kind of crazy bear garden? Not their lead-up to a battle, surely? What had come over them?

He turned to Verica and was puzzled by her expression. He pointed in one direction. 'Women and children!' he exclaimed with shock.

Verica looked and was mystified at the tone of his voice. 'Of course, what of it?'

'By all the gods this is going to be a big fight!' he protested. 'They should not be anywhere near here!'

Now it was her turn to be astonished. 'Why on earth not? They have come to watch and to be near their fighters to help them if necessary!'

'Give me strength!' Cathus muttered to himself, then aloud he added, 'What happens when the Roman cavalry run amok?'

'They don't have any,' Verica told him confidently. 'Our scouts would have spotted them by now and just look at our vast numbers!' she marvelled.

Cathus took a very deep breath. If he could not make her understand, how could he hope

174

to change the opinion of the lady and her cousin? He bottled his impatience. 'Do you Britons always war with your non-combatants on hand?' He made himself ask slowly as he struggled to remain patient.

'It is our custom!' she explained, and wondered why he was being so very obtuse.

Cathus exploded. 'It is the most stupid custom I've ever heard of!' he snapped. 'War is for warriors only. Look over there—two oldsters and—'

Verica's irritation showed. 'That just means they felt lonely at home, so rode up to watch!' What on earth was eating him? There were times when their culture clashes became difficult. How dare he criticise us and our ways, she thought, with rising annoyance.

Cathus had not finished. 'Look over there! There's even a young mother suckling a baby!'

Verica swiftly retorted. 'Well who'd feed it if she left it at home—the cattle?' she snapped sarcastically.

'She should *be* at home!'

Verica slowly counted to ten before speaking again. 'Cathus, war to us is a family matter. The only people who stay at home are the sick and very old. Everyone else makes the effort to attend even if it takes weeks of travelling. Apart from the entertainment of it, all the people come to give moral backing to the fighters. It is considered their duty. From a practical point of view, these non-

175

combatants, as you call them, are invaluable to the fighters. There is still food to be cooked, clothing to be quickly repaired, weapons to be re-sharpened, horses to be looked after and doctored. The warriors don't have that. They exercise to keep themselves fit and to keep challenging the enemy verbally to lower their morale with fright.'

Cathus was speechless by now, because he realised she believed every word she had uttered. He looked around for the lady, saw her and stamped over. Jodocca turned, expecting him to congratulate her on this marvellous turnout of fighters. She threw a sharp look at Verica and noted her furious face. What was happening with these two?

Cathus did not bother with finesse. 'Lady! I know you saw the XXth on the march,' he began bluntly, open. 'How many females did you count?'

Jodocca blinked. 'Why, none!'

Cathus persisted. 'How many oldsters and non-combatants?'

Jodocca frowned. Where was this leading? 'None!' she had to admit.

'When Rome goes to war, it is with deadly serious intent. Every man in the Legion including cooks, medical staff and whatever is capable of fighting. There are no hangers-on. Just highly trained and deadly efficient soldiers. They move fast and remorselessly. They stop for nothing. They sledgehammer their way forward,' and he waved one hand.

Jodocca felt rising irritation. 'What are you driving at, Cathus?'

'Get rid of all these hangers-on!' he grated. 'These are useless and superfluous,' he waved, one hand pointing around. 'Lady, I know what I'm talking about. A Legion has cavalry on fast horses, right now hidden well away but ready waiting all the same!'

'Our chariots—!' she began.

Cathus snorted disparagingly. 'A handful only.' He almost stamped his foot with frustration. How could he make her see and understand? Jodocca went to turn and leave him with annoyance, then froze. A tiny inner voice niggled at her He was Roman bred and trained.

Could he be right? She bit her bottom lip as a sudden wave of doubt assailed her.

'Get rid of them all!' He turned. 'Get them up into those hills, out of the way at least. The cavalry will have a job to reach them there!' he begged passionately.

'I will think about it,' she said coldly and walked away. Spies had come in, giving detailed reports, one of which she had never expected. There were two Roman soldiers hidden nearby, but they had not been touched. Orders had been specific. Observe and report back. A neat description had made her flinch. One was Marcus! What was he doing observing all from a hill? There was a

177

new officer in charge of the Roman camp, which also baffled her. She considered Cathus's agitation. It was true there were fewer chariots than she and her cousin would have liked. Her mind continued to revolve, and she became distinctly uneasy. When would the Romans come? It would not be today now, too much time had passed, but they were not camped nearby just for exercise. Her instinct told her it had to be the next day. She went back again, over her bodyguard's objections and her unease grew. He was right, she told herself reluctantly, all the non-combatants must go up into the safety of the hills. She looked up at the sky and made an estimation of the time, but doubted whether she could prod any of them to leave this day.

The next morning Cathus had made his own personal decision. He found the storyteller and explained to him. 'Get my wife and take her away from here. Will you, please?'

Tristus look deeply into his eyes then slowly nodded. 'If she will come with me!'

Cathus saw his point and thought rapidly. 'Tell her you think it would be wise to ride out and collect some more herbs and dressings for the battle wounds, and that you are a poor chariot driver. Make an excuse, invent a little lameness and exaggerate a limping walk. Once you're in the chariot with her take the reins from her and drive like hell to the top of that hill, if necessary, the horse can bolt with you but get her away!' he ended passionately.

Tristus stared deep into his eyes and nodded understandingly. With a better feeling in his heart, at least in that direction, Cathus hurried after Jodocca. They exchanged penetrating looks, and she pulled a face and nodded.

'I've spoken to my cousin. We will start to get rid of them at dawn. It's too late in the day now.'

'Tomorrow will be the day,' he said, knowing the Roman mind so well. 'What is your battle plan?'

'The chariots will go and cut them up, then we will go in and finish then,' she grinned. 'They will have to come towards us, and the flat ground to left and right will be perfect for the chariots. It's far too rough and stony in the centre, not just for wheels, but marching men!'

Cathus shook his head again. 'Wrong!' he said bluntly. 'You excel at the guerrilla tactics, but in a set piece battle—' He shook his head. 'That piece of rough ground will be nothing, because all legions practice for such. Each man will have a free hand, and with that he will grasp his neighbour's belt, and it is thus they will support each other as they continue to march, and I'm afraid you'll find them unstoppable and impregnable. The men at the front will have a shield in front of them, those at the sides likewise and those in the middle will hold a shield over their heads. It's called a testudo, which means a tortoiseshell. Every man inside is impregnable, and yet the flanks will still be capable of unleashing lethal weapons to take out all the chariot drivers.'

Jodocca considered his words. They rang with a nasty truth, and she bit her top lip. Before she could put forward a convincing argument he spoke again.

'And another thing, Lady! The Romans will be fully rested, marching under complete discipline, but your warriors? I know what they're going to be doing. Prancing around, waving their weapons, shouting personal challenges, exhausting themselves and their horses before they even deliver one blow. Lady, your battle has been lost before it has even started, I am very sad to say,' he ended heavily.

Jodocca was quietly appalled, went to argue, thought better of it, then looked helplessly at her bodyguard. 'I can't alter anything now. Everyone is too worked up for the fight, they would ignore me.'

'You can start to get rid of the non-combatants today,' Cathus told her, and explained what he'd done regarding the safety of his own wife.

'Run away?'

He understood her pride. 'Run away to stand and fight another day!'

'There is not a thing I can do about the fight. My cousin likes time to mull things over. The other tribal chiefs would be scornful. Tomorrow we have to make our stand once and for all.'

Cathus looked at her rather sadly. Was it any wonder that so much of this island was already under Roman domination?

Jodocca turned and walked away, very thoughtful. His words had alarmed her more than she had let on. She cursed herself soundly. She should have worked all this out and persuaded Caratacus to this new way of thinking but that was the trouble. It was all far too new to be immediately acceptable. She gave a deep sigh of misery. In battle tomorrow there would be no chance at all to settle the geasa.

*   *   *

Marcus and Crispus also knew that the next dawn would be battle day. Both of them had carefully prowled the previous evening, while there was still light. They had found nearby hoof prints, which were fresh and also foot prints, where someone had stood and observed them. So why hadn't these British scouts come back with reinforcements to attack them? They had mulled over the puzzle and deduced the real fighting was being saved for the battle but it certainly meant that they would have to change their position.

They arose very early, just as the sky was turning a delicate pink in the east. It would turn into a sunny day later on, excellent fighting weather.

'They are going to be massacred,' Crispus commented and Marcus gave a sigh of agreement. He wondered where *she* would be? Crassus was the officer commanding, and he could hardly go and get involved now. He cursed the geasa, plus female obstinacy. All those who were not killed and who were still sound of wind and limb would be taken prisoner, kept under very tight control and taken south and sold as slaves. If that happened, he knew he would buy her though how he would cope and manage to deal with her afterwards, with her natural stiff-necked pride, would be one enormous problem.

'Listen!' Crispus said quickly.

Marcus nodded his head. The Romans were on their march, heading for war, and, as always, they had been encouraged to burst into song as they marched in step. It was the first and favourite cadence.

'Sky, earth, road, stone
Steel cuts—to the bone!'

It would not be long before they shouted something more earthy and sexual. He felt his heart throb with pride. What a splendid sight

182

they made and he flashed a look at Crispus who was nodding his head in time to the marching boots. They exchanged a deep look, when each acknowledged they should have been down there with these marching soldiers. Then, both men turned to watch the British. It was crazy to watch them. Fighters milled around in tremendous activity with horses already sweating heavily. The warriors shouted, waved weapons and behaved in a totally uncontrollable manner. The horses which pulled the chariots were agitated with all the uproar, half-rearing, skippering sideways, only just under control with each driver struggling frantically at the reins. Each chariot had one warrior inside, who was forced to cling on frantically to keep his feet.

'Crazy!' Crispus grunted and Marcus agreed.

The Romans reached the rough ground and continued inexorably, not breaking step. Even when they went into a testudo.

Caratacus waved one hand, and the British hurled themselves forward, confident in their vast numbers and, once within range, the soldiers on each flank hurled weapons before replacing their shields, and it was mayhem. The few chariots, promptly out of control, crashed into each other and, with drivers wounded or dead horses, galloped headlong over the rough ground. Wheels were shattered, horses came down, and within a few heartbeats this little mobile division was totally obliterated.

The Britons flung themselves forward against the impregnable Romans, and they began to die. Within a few minutes, the keen warriors of the island had used up their remaining strength, and the Romans simply steam-rollered over them implacably.

Cathus kept close to Jodocca's side as she attacked from a flanking position. He stabbed and thrust, and struggled to keep an eye on her as she ducked and parried herself. Suddenly, the lead officer, no doubt attracted by the golden torque around her neck, started to lunge forward, his intent very obvious. It was bedlam with the screams and bellows, the clash of metal upon metal, horrific the way the ground changed colour from a delicate green to the dark red of blood.

Jodocca fought like a wildcat, saving her life every few seconds with the speed of her sword arm, the dexterous use of her shield and the uncanny ability of guiding her horse with knee and body movements alone.

*   *   *

Cathus knew this could not last for more than a few more seconds. He drove his frightened horse forward, intercepting blows and came head on with Lucius Crassus. Each recognised the other instantly, and both struck out at the same time. Cathus was the more desperate to get his lady out of this mêlée. All Crassus could think about was taking her his personal prisoner, which would enable him to crow beautifully over Gaius. His reflexes were just a heartbeat too slow and the javelin of Cathus severed the great neck artery on the right. Blood fountained in a huge gush, and now Cathus made his decision. Somehow he managed to sheath his javelin, swing his horse in a violent swerve, which brought him alongside his lady. With his powerful right arm, he snatched her around the waist, spun his horse around, and, without hesitation, bolted from the field of battle.

Jodocca was initially frozen with shock, then, when she realised what was actually happening, she writhed and screamed savagely but was held by his incredibly strong right arm. He took no notice of her at all.

Cathus rode like a mad man, but his horse found it heavy going with two to carry, especially Jodocca, who dangled down its flank, kicking and wriggling in rage. The horse struggled up the slope, labouring heavily, nostrils distended with effort, then Cathus knew she was going. Even his powerful biceps were exhausted. She fell at the top of the hill, landing heavily, while he also half fell, half dismounted from sheer fatigue.

'You! You!' she spat at him, and struggled for her dagger, as she staggered to her feet, face scarlet with fury and blood.

Cathus stood still, with head held high. Was this where it was all going to end? He knew he had acted correctly. He loved Verica, dearly, but beg for his life. Never!

As Jodocca lurched forward, murder in her eyes,Verica jumped first, a spear levelled menacingly.

'You do, and I'll run you through!' she snarled, and Jodocca halted with absolute shock as Tristus appeared. Where had the wishy-washy Verica gone? This blazing-eyed female was a wildcat. Tristus jumped. He never hesitated. He brought round a large right hand and smashed it against Jodocca's left cheek. She lurched with the blow's force, then fell backwards on her seat, immensely shocked, eyes darting from one to the other.

'Control yourself, Lady!' Tristus told her coldly. 'This man has brought you out of mortal danger and saved your life! Do not make a fool of yourself. The battle has been lost. Think about what your wise old grandfather would have said.'

Jodocca was stunned and almost speechless. Her face twisted miserably, and she felt horrible tears hovering. To think that Verica had been quite prepared to run her through was another shock; then she eyed her bodyguard's proud stance as he coolly and calmly awaited his fate. She also felt considerable humiliation.Very slowly, she stood, sheathed her dagger and took a deep breath. She did not have to be told what to do now.

'I apologise to all of you. Cathus, I owe you and this is now the second time. Verica, your husband is indeed a man. Storyteller, it sticks in my throat but it's true. We are no match for Romans in our present undisciplined state. I hate to say this though!'

Tristus smiled his approval at her natural honesty. Verica lowered her spear but prudently kept it by her side while Cathus allowed himself to relax. They all turned and looked downwards. It was just about all over. There were British bodies everywhere, while those who were still able struggled to flee. The Romans were enthusiastically killing all those who were too wounded to be patched up and sold as slaves while in the distance the cavalry had already started their own cleanup.

Tristus touched her arm. 'There is no time for any more speechmaking. We are in very plain view. It might be more politic to remove ourselves to a safer region,' he pointed out wisely.

Jodocca gasped. What was wrong with her? Had her wits become addled? She swallowed heavily and turned to Cathus.

'Three auxiliaries coming up the hill,' he cried in warning. 'Lady, we must have those horses!'

Jodocca flogged her brains back into action.

'Stand around with heads hanging as if we are beaten,' she snapped, then, slipping back into leadership once more: 'Cathus, take the man on your left. Verica, can you jump up and spear the middle one while I take him on the right?'

Verica nodded. She was worried sick about Kei but first things came first. They must get to safety, but the horses were vital.

They quickly composed themselves into a helpless subdued group with Tristus at their rear, and highly alert. The auxiliaries thundered up, shouting with glee, mocking these fresh prisoners. Two women and young ones as well. They could become prisoners after they had provided some sport while the two men were suitably restrained.

If they had been pure Romans they might have been more cautious, but they were from Gaul and still only half-trained. As they pulled their horses to a halt and slid off their backs, Jodocca moved first. Cathus and Verica were only a heartbeat behind her. It was a quick, bloody and efficient kill.

Jodocca mounted and Cathus and Verica did the same while Tristus awkwardly scrambled upon the back of the horse he had previously removed from the chariot.

'Now let's ride and get away from here!' she cried but Cathus dismounted again, and, going from body to body swiftly collected the weapons and handed them out, then vaulted

188

back onto his horse again. Jodocca berated herself. She should have thought of this herself. What was wrong with her? She had no idea she was in shock. Too much had happened too quickly and too disastrously for her to go back to thinking straight.

They set off in a controlled trot to conserve the animals' strength. Tears streamed down Jodocca's filthy face, and she shivered. Cathus eyed her and threw a warning look at his wife.Verica was quick on the uptake, and so was the storyteller. Their leader, so strong and controlled and dominant, was just about as helpless as a child.

They headed towards the sun and, very gradually, came across others who had managed to escape. It was with considerable relief and tears of joy that Verica found her son. Kei was battered and to a certain degree blooded, but his wounds were superficial. Jodocca questioned other survivors and was dismayed to learn two of the rest of her bodyguard were dead and one taken prisoner destined for slavery. Of Caratacus and his family there was no news at all.

Jodocca's tears gradually ceased, as she regained total control and started to consider the options available. They were not good. It was obvious that an attempt to go back home, so soon after fighting Romans, would not be a prudent move. Yet information must get to Macha for her mother's peace of mind. She eyed Kei. He was the one person who would be able to sneak through and get past the fort. Gloucester would be a problem with their old chief resident there but a young, quick moving boy, suitably briefed, might just be able to manage. She resolved to speak to him and Verica that evening.

As to their little group they could really only take refuge on the Silures' land. She had a deep gut feeling that, despite any forts the Romans might build, such wild land would be extremely difficult to conquer completely. It was even possible she would have to winter with the Silures. It would be a place for all of them to lick their wounds, to recover and be refreshed, to plan a new campaign for the spring and to rebuild themselves mentally.

TWELVE

Marcus looked around with worry and Crispus gave a little shake of his head. It was obvious he was looking for that wretched girl but he stifled a sigh of impatience and continued to follow his friend past the long line of British bodies. There were so many of them too. It had been more than a massacre; nothing but pure slaughter.

The Roman dead were not all that great in number, and they soon found Lucius Crassus.

190

Marcus studied him soberly. That one wound had been expert and lethal. From where they had been observing on the side of the hill, he had watched it all unfold. His eyes were younger and keener than those of his companion and Jodocca had been simplicity itself to identify because of her golden torque.

Marcus had watched Crassus fighting his way toward her, and his heart had risen to his mouth with fear. Then he had nearly applauded aloud as a British warrior dealt Crassus that horrendous blow. A few seconds later, he had seen Jodocca snatched from her horse's back by the warrior who had turned and ridden like a maniac to get her away from this slaughter. A little smile touched his lips as he imagined her fury and helplessness as she dangled by the horse's side.

Crispus was studying his features. 'I saw as well!' he confirmed then he continued. 'And I also saw who took her! It was our deserter, may he rot in hell!'

Marcus was surprised at that. He had been far too busy watching the drama with Jodocca to pay much attention to the man. At least, she had been taken well away from all this, and quite a distance too, otherwise she would have come back to join in again. Even her mother had admitted she had a knuckle-headed temperament when provoked, which could rarely be reached with reason.

'Are you quite sure it was our deserter?'

Crispus growled. 'It was he and one day I'll have a reckoning with him!'

'Well,' Marcus said slowly, 'there's nothing else to be done here. I'll have to go back and report to our dear governor, and then—' He paused and turned to Crispus. 'And then, come hell or high water, I'm going after her as a civilian to settle this ridiculous geasa and persuade her to become my wife!' he vowed harshly.

Crispus rolled his eyes with total exasperation but had sense enough to keep his feelings to himself. It looked as if he had been landed with a lot of future riding, in what would prove to be a very strange area of this island. Because although Marcus was protected against all Britons by this crazy geasa, he had no intention of letting him go alone. At the back of his mind was the itch to get hold of the deserter.

They slowly rode back southwards, through Gloucester and headed towards the fort. For himself Marcus felt strangely at peace in this area, which he had even begun to think of as home. When he reported to Scapula, he found hint in quite a benign moment.

'So now you leave us to become a civilian, but with the departing rank of Senior Tribune. I just hope you know what you're doing, wanting to settle on this confounded wet island with these barbaric savages,' he growled. 'It is that female, isn't it? Her and her stupid geasa! I thought you had more sense, man! Well, collect what's due to you and get out of my sight. I've enough on trying to run this country without dealing with besotted tribunes!'

Marcus was astounded. Scapula had almost been affable, but that wouldn't last long. The man was a very bad colour, and he had lost a lot of weight. He had sharp enough insight to realise that Publius Ostorius Scapula might not be long for this life. He gave a tiny shake to his head, suddenly quite relieved to be out of it all. He hoped Crispus felt exactly the same because it would be good to have such a reliable companion, a little bit like an older brother.

Outside Crispus awaited and grinned as he appeared. 'Well, well!' he chortled. 'I hear you are going out in a blaze of glory, Tribune!'

'Stuff you!' Marcus told him amiably. 'Get your horse—we are going down to that vill!'

'Tribune!' was bellowed at him, and turning he was astonished to see Scapula beckoning him back. 'Courier just came in with some excellent news. I thought it would interest you!'

Marcus froze uncertainly and flashed a look at his companion. Scapula intercepted it.

'No, no!' he barked. 'It's nothing to do with female warriors. It's much more important than that! Prince Caratacus has been taken prisoner, with all of his family. He must have panicked because he turned to our client Queen Cartimandua for help, and she promptly betrayed him to us. She knows which side her platter is flavoured after our latest victory. That's another thorn in our flesh removed.'

'She betrayed a fellow Briton? How low can you get! One day that woman will face a reckoning, and I would not like to be in her boots!'

Scapula bridled at this. 'She used her head more like! Without us Romans to back her up she would not even be a queen! I think you had better be on your way shortly, Tribune. It is crossing my mind that you are so besotted with this stupid female, that your wits have become addled and you are certainly no more good to Rome!'

Marcus gave him a hard look. 'You may just be right, sir!' he said in a voice heavily tinged with pure sarcasm, then he spun on his heel and strode away furiously, making Crispus hurry to catch up.

*   *   *

Both of them were thoughtful as they rode into the vill and they were both caught unawares. Another incoming rider was in a similar state of unpreparedness, coupled with exhaustion, and hunger. Macha was distracted with worries about the vill and coming to the

194

rapid conclusion that being chief was not all it was cracked up to be. Sellus was, as usual, wandering around giving a hand here and there with the animals or helping to reinforce a fence.

So it all happened at once, and the five of them froze with shock initially. Marcus and Crispus halted their horses to dismount. Kei heeled his nearly blown animal in from another direction. Sellus gawped in total surprise while Macha actually jumped with shock. The four of them looked in total confusion, but Kei was the first to react. With his youth's speed he flung himself from his mount before it could founder on to him, and prepared to bolt. Crispus was nearer and reacted more quickly.

He jumped forward, grabbed the boy by one arm, hurled him on the earth, twisted the arm in the socket and Kei froze in pain. Marcus jumped down and strode forward. Sellus blinked while Macha shot into a run, reached Crispus, and let fly with her right hand. Not only was she a very strong woman, but she also had the advantage of surprise. Her blow was also a very lucky one. It crashed into the jaw of Crispus and he staggered in his tracks, releasing Kei who struggled to his feet, intent on bolting again.

'Freeze!' Marcus bellowed in Latin and whipped out his javelin, his intention clear if anyone dared to disobey.

Macha turned on him, spitting fire and fury, kicking his bronze greaves, totally unimpressed by his javelin. Crispus dragged a short rope from his belt, jumped forward, grabbed the boy again before he could force exhausted legs into motion, and in a trice had him with hands tied behind his back. Marcus gave an impatient shove and sent Macha staggering sideways.

Sellus leaped forward now. 'You leave my woman alone, you big thug!' and, stepping sideways, he drove a balled fist from the rear into one of Marcus's kidneys.

Marcus winced badly, taken completely by surprise and astounded that a mere ex-ranker dared lay a hand on his person, let alone hit him. 'Why you—!' he swore lustily. 'Hitting me, an officer. I'll have you—'

Sellus cursed him back. 'You will do nothing to me, a civilian. If you know what's good for you, Gaius! Instead, you can go and get yourself well and truly stuffed, because if you lay one more finger on her, you'll regret you ever saw this Vill!' he snarled.

Macha was astounded at the look on his face, at his reaction and at everything about him. This was not the doddery old Sellus who quietly helped around. This was a stranger and a sudden respect shot sky high. There was a look on his face that boded ill for any man, Roman or otherwise, who thought about crossing him right now. This was indeed a very new Sellus, and she beamed with approval. Marcus collected himself and surveyed everyone including numerous interested spectators, as well as the goggle-eyed elders. Slowly a grin appeared on his face as the situation tickled his amusement. Weapons were slowly lowered and Marcus turned to face Macha and Sellus. 'Actually, I came in peace with the best of intentions, and I didn't think I'd need to battle here!'

Macha was first off the mark. 'Then let that boy go right now. Can't you see he is exhausted, and at the end of his tether? Get your hoodlum to release him. Now!'

Marcus gave a nod and Crispus removed the restraints and, still a little roughly, pushed Kei towards Macha. 'Go to Mother then!' he mocked.

Marcus eyed Macha who was ready to explode again; she must be flat-footed once more. 'What kind of a chief are you? Look at this boy. Ragged, filthy and hungry. Why haven't you seen to his welfare? I consider you a disgrace, woman! Now get about your duties!'

Macha was struck dumb with shock. Too astounded to protest. 'Me?' was all she managed to get out. Crispus smothered a grin. Marcus was an expert at doing this. Sellus stood bemused while Kei looked from one to the other uncertainly.

Marcus half turned and noted that some of

the Britons now had their hunting weapons with them. He turned the full force of his personality upon them.

'And you lot can get about your business as well!' he barked in his officer's voice. 'The fun is all over!' and he held his breath. Would they obey?

Slowly and with some reluctance the Britons dispersed uncertainly, and what might have become an inflammatory situation was quickly defused. Macha returned in a scurry with food and drink, while Sellus produced a stool . . .

'Now sit, boy, eat and drink and take your tinie,' Marcus said slowly, injecting kindness in his voice. The boy was like an unbroken colt. He needed gentling. One harsh word, and he would be up and off again.

Kei slumped wearily while he ate. He had never felt so tired in all his life, and he was heartbroken. The ride from the battlefield had been horrendous. He had not dared to come through Gloucester, which had added miles to his route. He had been terrified at night by all the spirits, which everyone knew were around, because he did not know the difference between good and bad. He'd really wanted his mother, and felt so lost without her—she was so far away. He was homesick for her and felt like a little boy again, not a budding warrior. He ate only because he knew he must rebuild his strength. He threw a warning look at Macha. He had so much to tell her, and how could he with these Romans here?

'This boy wants to talk to me privately,' Macha snapped impatiently. 'You are interlopers here, and not wanted!'

'We mean no harm.' Marcus tried to placate.

'Gloating then?' Macha challenged, which told Marcus she already knew what had happened, though probably minus the details.

'You think that of me then?' he asked somewhat sadly.

Macha had the grace to flush. He had been the one who had taken the trouble to send a warning message for Jodocca. Once again, he had made her feel a fool. What did it take to best him? Sellus stood near her protectively and one of his hands rested on her shoulder and squeezed.

Marcus nodded to her home. 'I wish to speak with you privately as well,' he told her. Macha flashed a sudden look of worry then led him forward. Sellus half went to follow but Crispus shook his head warningly. He dithered a moment, then complied but with reluctance.

Inside, Marcus took her right hand gently. 'Your daughter is alive. She survived and escaped the mopping-up operations.'

Macha's left hand flew to her throat. 'Oh!' she gasped, her eyes opening wide. 'Are you sure, really sure?'

So he told her all that he had witnessed. She heard him out, then sank on to a stool, shaking her head with relief and feeling the prickle of tears.

'Do you know where she is right now?'

He shook his head. 'I've no idea,' he told her, then grinned. 'But I think, wherever she is, she'll be in a real temper. Dragged off the battle field like that!'

Macha gave him a slow smile of agreement. 'Yes, she would indeed be a wild cat. Her pride would be hurt. But who was the warrior?'

Again he explained with the few facts he had. 'I do have some other news which you won't like. Caratacus and all his family are prisoners. They were betrayed by Cartimandua. They with the rest of the prisoners will soon be starting for Rome.' He stood slowly. 'I'll send Sellus into you,' he offered. 'He's a good man, you know!'

She nodded and blinked. She was elated with some of his news but despondent with the remainder. 'Thank you, Marcus Gaius. And what about you? Where do you go?'

He told her 'I'm just another civilian now and when I find where Jodocca has gone I intend to follow and pursue in order to press my suit!' He paused. 'To the ends of the earth if necessary!'

Macha stood and looked up at him. 'I think

maybe I was wrong about you after all, Roman, but my daughter will be a handful for any man,' she warned slowly.

'I'll chance that!' he laughed, and left her. Outside he turned to Sellus. 'Go in to her. She's had mixed news. Good and bad!' He nodded to Crispus as they mounted.

'I don't think we're exactly flavour of the month,' Crispus told him nodding at some of the Britons who loitered a little too near to their hunting spears.

'We've never been anything else!' Marcus replied a little shortly. 'That's the penalty of being Roman-born I'm afraid! I want a discreet eye keeping on that boy. Let him come and go as he likes. He will lead me to her . . . Let him trade for a horse in the future but not too soon, then make sure one of its hooves is marked for tracking purposes. Keep a sharp eye on him in and around Gloucester. He'll be back here again before winter, then probably go back again to winter wherever she is.'

Crispus eyed him a little glumly. 'What about that geasa?' he asked bluntly.

'I'll deal with it when *that* situation happens to arise!'

THIRTEEN

The weather became atrocious. The rain started as a gentle drizzle, then increased steadily, and within a short space of time they were all soaked to their skins and thoroughly miserable. It was impossible to stop, camp and make a fire for hot food. They had to keep riding, no matter how they felt, because they were uncertain how far behind were roving auxiliaries.

They picked up some other beaten warriors, and among them was a very subdued Llyn. He had been lucky to escape with superficial arm wounds. Jodocca brightened at seeing a familiar face as he rode alongside her.

'It was a murder,' Llyn said heavily. 'With our vast numbers we should have rolled over them.'

Jodocca had also been thinking on those lines, and she shook her head sadly. 'No, it's not numbers that count. It's how the fighters are organised and trained. We were like small children against those Romans, and I have a gut feeling that does not bode well for this island . . . They have four legions here, spread around nicely, and it appears there is very little we can do against them.'

Llyn considered this appraisal. It had the

ring of truth, even though it stuck in his throat. 'What do you plan now, Lady?'

Jodocca gritted her teeth. 'At this moment there is nothing I can plan which would be productive. We have to recover from this defeat. We have to regroup, and we have to plan more carefully and change our tactics to match those of the Romans.'

Would that ever be possible, she asked herself honestly? The Roman way of fighting was contrary to the British psyche. Their generations of tribal warfare meant they were naturally undisciplined and disunited. To wield them into one cohesive fighting unit that could act together under specific orders seemed a complete pipe dream—an absolute impossibility, which thought warned her they were doomed to a total Roman occupation.

'There is one way though that we can make Roman lives a misery and that is with guerrilla warfare. We are better at this than them, because we know the lie of the land better,' she thought, trying to marshal coherent ideas, 'but they will only ever be pinpricks. Never enough to drive them from our shores'

'Where do you ride now, Lady?' Llyn wanted to know. He had seen her fighting earlier from the corner of his eye, watched her bodyguard scoop her on his horse and then gallop to safety. It was an act of which he thoroughly approved, because, even then, Llyn had felt in his bones this day was not going to be theirs. Good leaders were too valuable to be wasted unnecessarily.

Cathus took the lead. 'We must find shelter!' and he pointed. 'There's some kind of a cave. At least we can get out of the cold a bit!'

Jodocca followed, still subdued. Too much had happened which had really shattered her confidence and she was so cold and hungry. Verica lolled miserably in the saddle, desperately missing Kei but it had been vital someone ride home with the news. Llyn rode all huddled up, trying to tell himself he was quite all right. Only Tristus was his usual self. He had been through so much misery in the past that little could really touch him now. Just to be alive and sound of wind and limb was bonus enough. Physical discomfort was merely something to be endured. As all that was good ended, so would everything that was bad.

It was almost dark as the five rode weary horses to a cave's entrance and flopped down, staggering from too many hours astride. Cathus had rapidly checked against wild animals, then came out later and scouted around on foot. They should be as safe here as anywhere for the night. They swiftly fastened loose rope hobbles then allowed the horses to go loose and graze.

It was the people who went hungry. A swift search of their possessions revealed only a little dried meat to be shared, which seemed to increase their appetites.

They hunkered down inside the cave to spend a miserable night. Cathus looked around. With flint and tinder plus some dried kindling found at the back of the cave, he had managed to persuade a small fire to burn. It held no warmth whatsoever, its value being purely psychological, because they could see each other a little as they huddled together trying to warm each other.

'Lady, this cannot go on like this,' Cathus said firmly, addressing Jodocca. 'We must have some plan of action and campaign. We must get food into our bellies.'

Jodocca knew he was perfectly correct, but where to go? It would be most unwise to turn around and head back south to the Dubonnii land. It would be far too soon after their defeat. The Romans would be cock-a-hoop, and that dreadful Scapula was perfectly capable of anything. This weather was unseasonably cold so did that mean winter was going to be early? She acknowledged that where downright campaigning was concerned Cathus was the expert. She lifted her eyebrows in a silent question.

Cathus understood, and he turned to Llyn. 'Are we far from your tribal lands?'

Llyn had to think hard and chew his lip while he calculated. 'Less than a week's riding,' and he eyed Cathus. 'I know what you're thinking, and I agree. Why don't you all winter with us Silures? You'll be as safe there as anywhere because Scapula might find it a little more difficult to exterminate us than he thinks. Our land is hilly and rough. Even if the Roman Pioneer Corp does start to build a chain of forts they are going to have a very bad time. That I promise!' he vowed.

Verica spoke suddenly, voicing her one great worry. 'That's all very well, but how is my son to find me again? It's going to be difficult enough for him, as it is!'

Cathus turned to her reassuringly. 'Kei is quite a remarkable tracker, for his age. He has a natural flair, and he's much better at it than me. He'll circle round the battlefield, then move over the hills checking. It won't take hint very long to find hoof prints, in a group, heading purposefully away from the battleground. He'll follow, and then scout to make sure we are the group he wants. He'll find his way to this cave, he'll see the ashes of this fire, and in no time at all he will appear and announce himself.'

Jodocca sat silently, well aware that the leadership had passed from her to Cathus. For a few seconds, she felt distinct annoyance, then castigated such childishness. It had always been the custom and rule that the best person led and who really was more suited to wage war against the Romans than another Roman?

Tristus sat in silence, letting his gaze rest upon one face, and then another. These people were so guileless it was simplicity to read their emotions. He had felt momentary jealous vibes shooting from Jodocca, but these had not lasted long and he nodded approvingly, catching her eye and she had blushed pink as if verbally complimented.

Cathus also let his gaze travel from face to face after a steady look at Jodocca. He was perfectly well aware the crown of authority now rested on his shoulders alone. It crossed his mind in a flash of surprise that if he had stayed in the legion, he might one day have made an officer also. Certainly, the authority of command rested easily with him.

Llyn admired Jodocca more than he could express in words, but deep down he had a stripe of pure male chauvinism. He acknowledged willingly that in hand-to-hand fighting he was no match for Jodocca. She would wipe the floor with him. Her speed and incredible reflexes far outweighed his superior muscle power. But, in Cathus, he sensed instinctively a latent leadership quality only now just coming to the fore.

Verica was totally disinterested in all these complex human emotions. She desperately wanted her son and was worried to death he would never find them. She considered the words of Cathus to be purely placatory. What she wanted was her son by her side.

All of them catnapped through a long, cold and very hungry night. Cathus, aroused first, plodded outside to make sure they were still alone and immediately spotted the small herd of deer not far away—four hinds and one stag, whose antlers showed he was neither old nor experienced. He crept back into the cave, caught Llyn's eye and silently showed him. They both calculated the distance to the nearest hind, then picked up their weapons and crept out very silently. They were fortunate the wind was in their face, and the immature stag only looked ahead and not to his rear.

With incredible stealth, they slithered over the ground until Cathus calculated they were within javelin range. Each looked at the other, exchanged a quick nod and stood to hurl their weapons. The hind had no chance at all and was dead before she hit the ground. With whoops of glee, they reached their kill, slit the throat to drain the blood, then hauled the meat back. The others in the cave had watched with bated breath, while Tristus, very practically, built the fire up, and then, with skilful fingers, arranged a roasting frame.

That of course decided them to spend another day and night there to eat and replenish their strength. Cathus worked out a simple rota system of one person being on guard outside all the time. Not that he expected Romans here—it was just his natural instinctive prudence.

With a comfortably full belly, almost wishing she could have a snooze, Jodocca took her turn on guard duty. She moved to a higher piece of land, which gave reasonable visibility and from where she could watch the grazing horses. She settled down, squatting on her heels, and eyed them. They were well fed now, relaxed and refreshed, ready to move on again.

Then her attention was attracted by her own mount, who suddenly stopped grazing, lifted his head and stared fixedly to her right. All the other horses then copied and Jodocca trotted back to the cave to catch the eye of Cathus.

'Something on my right has disturbed the horses,' she whispered.

He turned quickly, waved a hand for silence, then, grabbing his javelin, followed her, eyes everywhere. Was the intruder a carnivorous animal or a human? With hand signals that they had worked out previously, they separated, and moved forward silently in a pincer movement. Cathus padded around the corner of an animal trail then stopped, relaxed and smiled. A few seconds later, Jodocca joined him from another direction.

'I smell roast meat!' Kei said eagerly. 'I smelled it from ages away. Is there any for me? I am starving again!' he told them with a growing youth's constant hunger. 'I've spent ages getting here,' he grumbled. 'I followed four horse tracks. Then suddenly there were five, which threw me. I thought I had been tailing the wrong group, and I've been getting hungrier and hungrier!'

Cathus chuckled, and Jodocca smiled at the rueful look on his face. She led the way back to the cave, while Cathus examined the area to make sure that no one had trailed Kei.

As Kei entered the cave, Verica leapt up with a shout of delight and hugged him wildly. Kei tolerated this for a few seconds, then sniffed again at the appetising aroma while his mouth salivated with anticipation.

Verica sprang into action, and, with a sharp knife, chopped a hunk of the venison to give him, which he immediately started to wolf.

They all waited, forcing themselves to be patient, until his stomach was replete. He looked around and beamed and turned to Jodocca.

'All is well at home.' Then he paused. 'Well at least I think it is. Your mother is being courted hard. The man has had a few problems with her, but I think he is slowly winning. He's certainly worked hard enough at courting and people have been taking bets as to when your mother will yield. He is Roman, of course!'

Jodocca was dumbfounded at this news, then sat bolt upright. 'Roman!' she exclaimed. 'I don't believe it—not after what she said to me!'

Kei was highly amused at the disbelieving expression on the lady's face. 'It's a fact. His name is Sellus. He is out of the legion now, and plans to retire to wed your mother!'

Jodocca turned a stunned face to Cathus. 'Well, who is this man?' she barked.

Cathus grinned at the expression on her face. 'He was just an ordinary ranker like me, a bit older. He never drank too much. I never saw him gamble. He wasn't a bad fighter, but not a brilliant one either, because he had been injured. That's how he has managed to get an early discharge.'

Jodocca was speechless with it all. She shook her head with exasperation, so Kei decided to give her the rest of the news.

'That other Roman officer, the one who fancied you, Lady, the one with your geasa on him, was also at our home with his companion,' and he explained what had happened on his return. 'He went into your mother's home by himself and spent quite a time there. When your mother did finally come out she seemed a bit disturbed even though Sellus was with her.'

'What in Hades does he want now?' she growled. 'Once I've had my fight with him, he can take himself off anywhere else he likes, but he'll leave me alone if he wants to stay healthy!' she snapped.

Marcus Gaius was turning into a perpetual

thorn in her flesh. All of a sudden, for the first time, she was glad she wasn't in her home area. It certainly would be a beautiful escape to winter with the Silures. Once spring came, they could start a fresh campaign against the invaders, and the terrain would be on their side. Let the Romans build their forts, it would be a delight to destroy each one, and, as for Marcus Gaius, she would have her day of reckoning with him, come what may.

Kei was still not finished. 'Our old chief is dead. He suddenly collapsed in Gloucester; it was his heart. That means, Lady, a good day and a half can be cut from the journey time back home.'

Jodocca flashed a look at Cathus. 'That certainly would be useful,' she said, and then explained to Kei their plans for over-wintering. 'When you are thoroughly rested and feel like it, would you like to ride back home again, and explain to my mother and the elders what we are going to do and why?'

Kei nodded enthusiastically. He was thoroughly enjoying the importance of being their vital carrier and he knew, as a young boy, he was much below the attention of any Roman as long as he did not get into a row with one.

'There is one more bit of news but it is bad,' he said in a grave voice, and the rest of the little group stilled. 'Prince Caratacus and his family managed to escape, and they took

212

refuge temporarily with Queen Cartimandua, who promptly handed them over to the Romans. It is most likely they are on their way to Rome right now, and bound for the slave pens.'

A heavy gloom descended upon the little group; only Tristus, not fully understanding the political and family implications involved, sat aloof. These Britons could be very passionate people, and he suspected they also had it in them to be revengeful. Exactly who this queen was he had not the slightest idea, but it occurred to him that her days as queen might be very numbered indeed.

'Any other news?' Jodocca asked. She felt sick at heart at the thought of her cherished cousin being turned into a Roman slave.

Kei nodded. 'It is rumoured that Scapula will be leaving the fort and heading back to Rome. He is a very sick man. There is a tribune in charge, right now, so perhaps when another governor is installed it will not be in our area. Perhaps somewhere like London?'

That did make interesting news. Was it possible that one day, she might be able to return to her tribal lands, Jodocca asked herself? Knowing that Roman legionnaires could march twenty-five of their miles in a day and fight and win a battle on top, there was really no need for any Romans to be at the fort, was there? Gloucester was therefore but a day's hard march away for fit Romans. It was an interesting thought, but she pushed it to the back of her head for later dissection.

* * *

Macha took the bull by the horns the following evening. Already the nights had started to get chilly, so she and Sellus were glad to sit around a generous fire in her home. Sellus had moved in with her, and they had delighted in exploring each other's sexuality. Macha had made quite sure that Sellus knew males and females were totally equal in a Briton's culture. This had been a little bit of a shock to him initially but now he was well used to the idea and just wanted to regularise their union once and for all.

'There is something I want to do in the spring,' she began, which made him wonder what was coming next. Macha seemed to be full of surprises. There was certainly nothing boring about her. 'I want to go and visit my daughter.'

Sellus was baffled. 'But she could be anywhere,' he pointed out.

Macha shook her head firmly. 'I know where she will be and I'm not telling you until we're married.'

Sellus gave a tiny grimace, shaking his head. He knew perfectly well the boy had played another flying visit, so obviously he had imparted this information. He opened his mouth to object to her secrecy, then snapped it shut again. He thought about the situation for a moment, then realised he could not keep silent.

'You don't trust me!' he said, a little sadly and rather hurt.

Macha realised she had gone perhaps a little too far and took his hand. 'I can't help being secretive,' she told him. 'I suppose it is more force of habit, because you are a Roman. Even when we marry, you have said you will not become a Briton.'

'No!' he said firmly. He would give up a lot for this woman but become a Briton he would not. 'I will compromise! I will become a Romano Briton. This breed does exist, because I've heard of them in other places,' he offered.

So had Macha and it did quite satisfy her. She took a deep breath and made up her mind. 'My daughter will be spending the winter with the Silures tribe. Their land is quite away from here. Far over the other side of the River Severn and it's high, wild and mountainous. The people are like their land, and now that it's fairly common knowledge Scapula wants them exterminated they are going to become even more aggressive and barbaric. We have inter-married with them at times and they make splendid fighters. That Roman edict might just rebound in Roman faces. Before people can be exterminated they have to be found and caught and that might be just a little easier said than done!'

Sellus realised he was totally ignorant about much of this island, especially concerning the lands the other side of that awesome and quite frightening River Severn.

'You are the chief here,' he pointed out steadily and opened his mouth to continue but she forestalled him.

'And I'm fed up with the position. It's not what I thought it was and I can see now why that fat old chief of ours was glad to walk away from the job. As to who runs this vill, the elders can. There are six of them sitting around on their backsides all day doing absolutely nothing at all. They can work out a rota system and earn their position of seniority. Why two of them are only a few years older than me. They can move off their rumps and do a bit of work themselves. We shall have an early winter, which should mean an early spring, and I intend to be off to see my girl, to see exactly what she's doing!' Then she grinned mischievously. 'I swore Kei to absolute secrecy, so that it will be a lovely surprise for her.'

Sellus was not at all sure about this. He knew that some people did not take kindly to surprises, but a look at Macha's face showed this would be an imprudent thought to offer.

'Do you know the way?' he asked a little dubiously.

'No,' she admitted reluctantly! 'But I have a tongue in my head, and I can ask questions with the best of them and if any stupid Roman anywhere tries to get difficult he will regret it!'

Although he was now a civilian, Sellus was far more up to date than Macha knew, because he still had Roman connections, which he intended to keep. There was no telling when gossipy information would be of use, although he had decided to keep this fact from Macha.

He was not particularly certain about the wisdom of her proposed spring venture. If only there were a safe and reliable way to cross the River Severn many days hard riding would be saved. He had heard that some very bold or foolhardy Britons had ventured onto the Severn in flimsy coracles. From the stories that had reached him more drowned than made the far side.

It was not just the width of the mighty river, but the vicious currents and unexpected whirlpools as well as the river's general highly erratic nature. To cross the Severn with any degree of safety at all it was imperative the traveller went as far as Gloucester at least.

As for himself, he was most uncertain how to navigate into this strange area and protect a woman at the same time. He kept his features impassive, so that Macha was unable to follow his line of reasoning and general worry. There was another point that bothered him, which he had also kept to himself. Although now an official civilian, he would certainly fall under official Roman rules and might possibly be called back as a reservist should a legion need sudden back-up troops. It was for this very reason that Rome encouraged its retired soldiers to settle on foreign lands, and not contemplate returning to Rome.

He chewed his lip thoughtfully, and wished he could discuss his situation with someone who would understand the politics of it all. The last thing he wanted to do was start wandering around into some strange tribe's territory and have Rome call him a spy for the British.

One thought, which had merely hovered at the back of his mind, started to push itself forward, energetically. Marcus Gaius! He could talk to him because he knew instinctively this retired officer would give sound advice. At the same time, he was well aware of the crazy British female's geasa, which meant Gaius had to meet her some day. He also had a very good suspicion that Gaius was still head over heels in love or infatuated with Macha's daughter.

Marcus Gaius was no longer around though, and with Crispus also retired, and his companion, soldiers' rumour had it that he was either at Cirencester, Gloucester or Bath. This would make an impossible amount of riding to find and reach him and what possible excuse could he give to Macha?

Problems and worries filled his mind and made him a little mentally abstracted. This did not escape Macha. What had come over him? Surely he was not getting cold feet at their proposed marriage? She began to withdraw into herself a little, immersed in her own small plans so, although they there had been no quarrel, the pair started gently to drift apart without a cross word between them.

*　　*　　*

He swore afterwards the goddess of love had favoured him because who should come riding into their area but Marcus Gaius and Crispus. It was so unexpected he nearly missed his opportunity.

Sellus had been depressed one morning, and Macha was in one of her tetchy moods so he had grabbed a hunting spear and gone out after game. He had deliberately gone alone, because he was so low in spirit, and with all his worries it would have been impossible to make affable conversation.

He rode further west than he had ever gone before, when he spotted two horses hobbled together under a clump of trees and the two Romans.

Marcus was studying the plans of a villa which he had had drawn up. 'This will be a good place,' and he waved one hand around. Crispus had to agree. It was perfect land for stock grazing, and it was possible it would avoid the worst winter blizzards. In a way he was very amused at the situation in general.

'Well, go ahead and build your villa. This is certainly a spot for a good home, and I might even follow suit. You never know, it's so good here a little town might even develop one day. But aren't you forgetting something? You still have to find and tame your hellcat, and I have no one in mind at all!' he grumbled.

Marcus grunted. 'Then keep your eyes open when we're riding around and you might find someone to suit. Hello! Who is this coming?' and he loosened his javelin, then relaxed, as he recognised Sellus. 'Well, you are a stranger soldier, and you look as if you've lost a pouch full of silver denarii and found only a few copper ones!'

Sellus dismounted and automatically went to salute, then realised how ridiculous that was for three civilians. His spirit brightened. This officer had always been a good one, and even Crispus was not bad for his rank.

'Sir! I'm very upset and very worried and I don't know what to do!' he blurted out in a rush of words, then stood, just a little pathetically, expecting immediate advice and help from someone who was of higher rank.

Marcus managed to keep the smile off his face and threw a glance of warning at Crispus.

This ex-soldier looked as if the end of the world was nigh. 'What's the matter, soldier, has your woman turned you down again?'

Sellus gave a weary sigh, shaking his head. 'Oh no, we're going to get married—it's what she wants me to do next spring. I don't want to be branded a spy by Rome, but I can't let her down or she'll think I don't really love her!'

Marcus sensed a convoluted story was waiting to be told, and even Crispus stepped nearer, so he wouldn't miss a word. 'Right, let's hear all your problems and I'll try and act as the shaman!'

Sellus opened his mouth and words flooded as he explained his dilemma without missing a single beat.

When he had finished, Marcus flashed a look at Crispus and their thoughts were identical. No wonder they had not heard from her, hidden away in a mountainous retreat— just about impossible to find if she wished to remain hidden.

'I bet those forts are finished by now,' he mused aloud. 'The powers that be would want that before winter set in. And what's the betting,' Marcus said slowly, to no one in particular, 'the Silures will wage war against them using their guerrilla attacks?' He paused. 'At least I know which way to ride to try and net her,' then a fresh thought occurred to him. 'Yes, yes, that will do quite nicely and solve a lot of problems in one stroke.'

Sellus looked blankly at him, totally lost. 'I don't understand you at all, sir!'

'That female, your intended's daughter, it's she whom I want for a wife but I had no idea where she had vanished to. It will still be tricky to find the specific place, but we have a nice bait, though you have to keep your mouth shut from now on,' he warned sternly.

Sellus would have promised anything to have his mind at rest. He nodded eagerly, so Marcus continued.

'I predict that once spring comes that young boy they use as a courier will be over here to see your woman. We'll let him go on his own way back through Gloucester and make sure he has a new mount with especially marked hooves for easy tracking. We will follow at a discreet distance behind—by we I mean us two and you and your woman. As a small self-contained, fighting unit, we should get through quite easily. What happens then will depend upon many factors, but we'll play those situations by ear. Can you see now why it is imperative that young boy learns nothing at all and your woman as well?'

Sellus turned it all over it in his mind and beamed with relief. Let Macha think it was just two of them until they met up with these Romans. It would be far too late for her to change her mind and go back, let alone have a tantrum. He grinned from ear to ear, with total relief.

'Satisfied, soldier?' Marcus asked. 'Well in that case, we all meet up early spring. When that courier is sure to appear. I will have people keep an eye open in Gloucester. When he rides south then you and your woman follow after him. Me and Crispus will meet you somewhere the far side of Gloucester so we can be together. Now clear off! These are the plans of what's going to be my villa, and I want to check them out for measurement, and I can't do that with you watching every step. Go!' he thundered and Sellus was more than happy to agree. He had to compose himself and his features before he saw Macha. She could be incredibly sharp and intuitive.

*   *   *

Jodocca watched Cathus and Verica and felt a stab of something and acknowledged with surprise it was jealousy. She examined her conscience and wondered just what was the matter with her. They were such a well-matched pair, almost deliriously happy in each other's company and she realised she felt quite incredibly alone at times. She thought a few seconds about Marcus Gaius, visualising his mesmeric masculine aura, and she scowled. It was certainly the worst day's work she had done when she bumped into him all that while ago. Because since that day nothing had gone right at all. He was nothing but bad luck for her. Was this what her grandfather had meant?

They were well into winter now, and comfortable enough in individual homes. Yet, when a foul blizzard did arrive, they were all perfectly free to move into a large mountain cave. Here there was always an enormous fire burning with rocks around covered with skins—they had as many seats as they wanted. This tribe knew how to make itself comfortable, and there was plenty of meat and food. She also liked these people. Once she had become more used to their rougher ways they were very good company.

It was true that it was difficult to keep clean, because no one wanted to strip off in this biting cold, and she often thought wonderingly about a hot Roman bath. That was the one object in their culture that she did admire.

What she did not like was this mountainous region in which a tree was so rare it attracted comment. Jodocca was a creature of more flat land, and green forests. She felt exposed here and she wondered if she would ever be able to return to her native land in safety.

Cathus had told her how he particularly liked a mountainous region. It was similar to where he had been born, and he was very comfortable in the Silures' territory. Verica of course was so much in love with him she would have followed him anywhere without hesitation.

The one great advantage of such territory was that when the weather co-operated they had excellent visibility across a huge distance. As the men and women of this tribe were hardy and rugged so were their animals. Their horses were a little smaller, but with hard-boned legs and hooves. They were incredibly surefooted on the rough terrain, with a stamina that meant they could be ridden for hours.

Chief Kersun ran a tight band. When quarrels arose, he would allow them to boil to a certain pitch before he stepped in to quieten everyone down. He was a good chief and Llyn took after him and would make a natural successor.

If any of them stood out it was she and Cathus. They were the total outsiders, just guests of this tribe. Tristus had integrated beautifully into this tribal life. Circumstances had made him adaptable, and he thrived. The people accepted him completely, even though they did still mock at his 'death on the cross'. It was totally impossible because of their aggressive natures for them to understand such a death without any fighting resistance. His storytelling though was so sincerely done that he suspected he was planting little seeds of the new religion, which would one day flourish. He was quite happy to work at whatever task was given to him and he always did this well. Jodocca could see that one day he would move into a senior position as a wise elder of this tribe.

One evening Cathus strolled over and sat down beside her. 'Lady, I have been doing a lot of thinking. You all adopted me and made me a member of the Dubonnii, but realistically, I will never be able to live there. Even with Scapula, and the numbers in that fort run down, I would always be in danger. Rome never forgives a deserter. With these people in a land that I like, I could make a good home and future for me and Verica and the child she is carrying. It's here I wish to put down my roots.'

Jodocca was not at all surprised at this. 'There is no problem there. Just explain yourself to Chief Kersun. He will be more than happy to have another warrior.'

Cathus nodded happily at this and then frowned again. 'But I am your chosen bodyguard,' he pointed out, 'and there are still those Roman forts in the area to say nothing of your geasa!' he reminded her.

Jodocca nodded. 'I want to take out those forts, and once the Romans rebuild them, as they will, then they will be taken out again. Surely even Romans will slowly get the message?'

'You will plan and lead us, Lady?'

Jodocca shook her head. 'Not me! You!

You will lead, but we will plan it altogether. Many heads are better than one.'

Young, hardy scouts had regularly ridden out to spy on the forts, and there was very little that the Britons did not know about the construction and internal layout, as well as the number of men garrisoned there.

Cathus considered. 'We all need numerous ladders for scaling the walls on all sides at once, and perhaps even a battering ram for the main gate,' he mused aloud. 'And these men must be made to obey orders, to do as they're told, and not to act as individuals. In other words, they must be made to copy Roman battle behaviour.'

Jodocca agreed. 'My sentiments exactly, so I suggest you and I both go and have a long chat with the chief and then all the warriors. You may have to stamp your authority upon them,' she warned with a grin.

'That will be a pleasure, Lady, so let's go and talk to Kersun now!'

Tristus missed nothing and although it had been too far away to eavesdrop on anything it did not require a lot of mental deduction to work out what was being planned. Soon all fighters were gathered round the chief, giving him their undivided attention. After that, it was the turn of Jodocca and Cathus to speak out. There were one or two objections from some of the younger members so without hesitation Cathus strode over and with a huge hard fist hammered the young rebels into immediate submission. It was the kind of physical language they understood and accepted.

'I am going to lick you lot into disciplined shape and the first one of you who just puts one toe out of line will wish he had never been born!' Cathus promised in a very even cold voice. 'Understood?' he barked. He was met with hurried murmurs of assent and head-nodding, which made both Jodocca and the chief exchange glances, nods of approval and, at the same time, smother very wide grins.

Although the winter was savage, it was mercifully short, and they were able to send Kei on one of his trips back home with all their news. He had become quite an expert and thrived as a result of his responsibility. While he was away Cathus worked hard at instilling battle discipline into the fighters. Initially, some did still resent this, quite unable to see the point, but Cathus was more than capable of making then change their minds with his fists. Others who were too old worked at making scaling ladders, which was no easy task in a land bereft of trees. Jodocca, Cathus and Kersun spent many hours planning tactics and strategy.

They were so engrossed in all of this they were astonished at their courier's return, and amazed at how quickly time passed. He returned in his usual ravenous condition, and internally was bursting to tell of Macha's imminent arrival but he managed to restrain himself.

'I have a splendid new horse, Lady,' he said, itching to share his cleverness. 'He's down with the rest of them.'

They kept the bulk of their horse herd in a nearby valley, which was sheltered and which had good grazing and water: easily accessible at all times.

Jodocca was puzzled at his excitement. 'You already have a good mount,' she pointed out and stood, throwing a smile at Cathus, 'so let's see what's special about this one!'

The three of them walked down to the small herd. Kei pointed enthusiastically. 'That bay!'

Jodocca and Cathus examined the animal, then exchanged a questioning look. Kei bubbled with glee.

'It all happened when I came through Gloucester,' he started to explain. 'There was a small horse fair, and I stopped to look and saw this wonderful creature. I went up and stroked her, so beautiful and so strong, and she looked so fast and powerful. I did so want her, Lady, and now I have her. I was able to haggle the price down, and the man who was selling let me have her pretty cheap. Isn't she marvellous?'

Jodocca exchanged a questioning look with Cathus. This horse was a little too marvellous for anyone to get cheap. 'Catch her and bring her over, will you, Kei so we can look at her properly.'

He sprang to obey, eager to show off this wonderful treasure. Again Jodocca and Cathus exchanged a puzzled look and when the young courier brought the horse they walked around examining it very carefully indeed. Jodocca stood thinking deeply. There was a smell to this that she did not like. With a flash of inspiration she bent down and lifted each front hoof in turn. Her nostrils flared and anger showed in the bleak look on her face.

'What is it?' Kei whispered with fright.

Jodocca gave a deep sigh of exasperation. 'Oh Kei! What have you done?!' She knew she could not get really angry with him because he was only a young boy, doing the best he could at all times. There was only one person at the back of this, and she almost snarled with anger.

She turned to face Kei and could see his distress. 'You have fallen into one of the oldest traps of the world, and I am the bait!' She turned to Cathus, nodded at the horses' hooves, so he bent down and picked them up to examine for himself.

Jodocca almost spat with anger. 'This is just another typical low-down Roman trick, aimed at me, I don't know what his game is now but he would do well to remember my geasa!'

Kei was utterly mystified and nearly in tears. Cathus drew him forward to show him. 'You were meant to buy this animal, and only ever this one. Each front hoof has a V-shaped nick, which makes it the easiest animal to track on the whole of this island!'

'But who, why—?' Kei gasped.

Jodocca was almost beside herself with fury. 'Let him just put one boot towards me, and he will find that what I did to Riothamus I can repeat on him!'

Cathus chewed his lip and had enough sense to keep his mouth shut. The lady in a temper was not one for reasonable argument. He still considered himself her personal bodyguard and he had a flashing realisation that if Marcus Gaius was indeed heading in this direction, he was going to have problems with the lady. She would fight him at the drop of a hat, but not if he could do something about it. The Roman officer would be more difficult and complicated than her old bodyguard.

Kei was distressed. Why hadn't he thought to check such a detail? He remembered the purchase and agreed that the bargaining had not been very severe. He should have suspected something.

Cathus turned to Jodocca. 'I'll take and ride this animal!'

'No! She's mine!' Kei protested hotly.

Jodocca laid a hand on his shoulder: 'Yes,

231

she is yours, but also let this be a lesson to you. If anything comes cheap ask why. However, in my position this quality animal is only fit for someone of my status. I'll rent her from you!' and she dived into her tunic, pulled out her little purse and handed some coins to Kei.

'But she is still mine, isn't she?' asked Kei plaintively.

'Yes, I've just rented her for a short time,' she reassured Kei, then threw a hard, challenging look at Cathus, before turning on her heel to walk away.

FOURTEEN

Jodocca turned to Cathus; they had gone over their plans time and again, honing small details until neither of them could think of another improvement.

'The men?' Jodocca asked Cathus.

He pulled a face. 'They have improved I must admit but they'll not make legionnaires yet. I think though, they are beginning to understand that a disciplined attack gives better value than one from a rabble. If we attack the first fort from both sides at once, and leave a reserve to try the gates we should not have any great problems. We'll move off in the middle of the night, so we can start a dawn attack. At that hour, everyone's defences will be down'

'I wonder where the other legions are,' she mused.

'The last I knew was that the IInd Augusta were at Exeter, the XXth based at Gloucester and the XIVth somewhere near the Brigantia region. It is possible the IXth are still around the Iceni region. King Prasatgus has shown he is amenable to Romans, though I have heard his Queen Boudicca is very hostile. She hates Romans, and as the king seems to be a very sick man I smell trouble coming there. Let her take over the reins of complete control, and it is quite likely the Iceni will rise up in revolt with her and attack London. With no legion there, they could cause enormous destruction and the whole country, except a few boot-licking tribal heads, would rise with her.'

She turned all this over in her mind. 'So, what this means is those border forts will have great difficulty in calling up reinforcements in a hurry.'

Cathus agreed. 'All of the various trades connected to legions are filled with skilled men, all of whom have first had to undergo basic military training. Like that which I went through. But none of then are what I call battle hardened. Especially men in the Pioneer Corps. They will fight of course, but they will be much less skilled.'

'If we attack the first fort at dawn, and if

you can retain control of the men, and not let them go whooping it up, we will ride straight on to the third fort. Leave fort number two to sweat it out. The same with fort number four,' she said firmly.

Cathus agreed completely. No man liked a surprise attack, when he was least prepared to put his life on the line. A border region in revolt was the last thing the new governor of Britain would want.

'Once the attack starts, I want Kei to ride off and reconnoitre the whole area for us and then we will know exactly where we stand,' she continued thoughtfully.

Cathus agreed and knew he had to hand it to her for brilliant tactical planning. He could not have done better himself and he flashed his teeth in a smile of approval at her. They made a very good team.

Later on Tristus strolled over to Jodocca. In his gentle, almost mellifluous voice, he studied her before he spoke. There was a hard mask on her face and he gave a deep sigh.

'It is settled then?' he asked gently. 'You go to war once more?'

'Of course! What else is there to do?' Jodocca riposted. She could sense his disapproval, but in her make-up pacifism did not exist.

Tristus could think of many other things to do, but forbore to tell her. He had developed a very fond attachment for this strong-willed female, much as he would have for a favoured granddaughter. He felt sharp worry for her safety despite what he had heard about her fighting ability and championship status. He was well aware that Cathus would be a perfect bodyguard, but he was distinctly uneasy about this geasa business. He was just grateful that the Roman in question was so very far away. He gave a tiny shrug to his shoulders, pulled a little moué, and walked away to go and talk to Verica. Was it his imagination that she had begun to show a genuine and sincere interest in his Christ story? Was it possible he was making her a true convert? His heart swelled with hope.

By now Jodocca had acquired a good local knowledge of the various trails, and she particularly liked one that ended on a very large and long flat rock. It was a platform, which made an excellent general lookout. On one side was the trail, but on the other, way down below, thundered a vigorous mountain stream. It leapt over and thrashed its boulder-strewn course at a fast speed, with fair depth and considerable white water. It had become a favourite look-out point, because, when the visibility was good, a huge distance could be surveyed.

She was always prudently cautious though not to get too near the side, which hovered over the stream, way below. The hillside downwards was a mixture of poor earth, scree and larger stones. It was within a reasonable riding distance of the tribal homes, and she sat on her horse there going over their plans for the final time. If *only* the men would stay disciplined and controlled, victory was guaranteed.

Under the watchful eyes of their two leaders, the fighting men approached the first fort in silence, then quietly split into two groups. Those who had to go the far side moved off, and as their horses' hooves had been muffled with cloth they made very little sound at all. The men with scaling ladders brought up the rear and Jodocca motioned everyone to keep still and silent, while she counted.

She and Cathus, who had worked out a waiting time of so many numbers, counted slowly. Once these were passed, she motioned the men with the ladders to be ready, and at that second she heard a warning crying from a Roman sentry. Jodocca waved away one hand imperiously and the ladder men ran forward. Everyone else had dismounted and the horses' reins were held by two older men.

Everything then happened at once. The ladders went up against the walls, fighters scaled them while a prearranged small group battled their way forward to open the gates. The reserve, with Jodocca leading, burst into what was a parade ground, and there was immediate hand-to-hand fighting. It was slaughter for the Romans. They had been taken completely unawares, and many, still half asleep, fought haphazardly. They had no chance at all. In a very short space of time the Romans were all butchered and immediately the tribes people went to break into one of their usual victory dances. Cathus and Jodocca were everywhere and by sheer force of personality, plus a few blows from their fists, these were stilled very rapidly.

'Outside, most of you, and mount up. You only just started! Someone set fire to this place and follow on behind. The next fort now, and it is a bit further to go!' she cried enthusiastically putting herself at the lead as Cathus joined her.

'Do you think any Roman managed to get away to sound an alarm?' she asked him, as they cantered forward.

Cathus shook his head. 'I don't think so, but if one did, he would go to the second fort, which is the nearest. If we can get to the third before a general alarm has been sounded that too should be easy, even without the ladders.'

They rode fast and by throwing scowling looks at the men behind they maintained a reasonable degree of quiet. The third fort stood more isolated, and the Romans were far more alert as dawn had long broken. The attackers divided into four this time, so each side was attacked simultaneously.

To compensate for no ladders, the men

swiftly formed a human one on each others' shoulders with the lightest and fastest men on top. This was more difficult for the Britons but their adrenalin was at a high pitch from the first victory. Once some men were over the walls others remained near the gates until they were forced open. The Romans fought valiantly, but again were overwhelmed. It was exactly as Cathus had stated. These were pioneers, tradesmen, not crack fighting troops. No prisoners were considered, and, once again, the Britons finished their work with fire.

Cathus joined Jodocca. Both were quite unscathed, but breathed a little hard from their efforts. They grinned at each other in jubilation smugly pleased with themselves.

'Now?' Cathus asked.

'Home!' Jodocca confirmed this part of their plans. It would be expecting much too much for the men to stay restrained for much longer. They were entitled to go home and celebrate wildly. But Jodocca and Cathus would then have to have a roll call to find out who had been killed, so their families could be told, and the injured shepherded to the care of Tristus and others who specialised in treating wounds. She turned and scanned the excited warriors. Nearly all had wounds of some kind or another, and a few, she knew from past experience, would be fatal. She was pleased to see Llyn had survived unscathed, though covered with blood—obviously Roman.

She exchanged a quick look of satisfaction with Cathus and he grinned over to her. 'That is going to give the Romans something to think about!' he chortled with immense satisfaction.

Jodocca nodded. She felt on a high that they had managed to obtain some bloody recompense for their last humiliating defeat. It was obvious the Romans would rebuild these forts again, and the next time they were attacked there would have to be a fresh strategy. It was a start though, and the Britons' moral was sky high—an emotion that had been needed desperately.

* * *

Marcus felt distinctly uncomfortable, and he pulled a face at Crispus. Macha was not a travelling companion he would have chosen. She had been awkward and hostile from the moment they had met to form the little group of four. He would have preferred it if she had ranted and raved at him but all she had done was eye him from head to toes with a cold glare, then she had cut him dead and ignored him.

Sellus had been apologetic, but helpless to get round Macha's frosty attitude. When they camped at night, each taking a turn on sentry duty, Macha had joined in. Marcus would have been quite happy to let her miss her turn but he did not quite dare to suggest this. An instinct told him Macha would not hesitate to turn on him.

'Like mother, like daughter!' he murmured, in a low voice to Crispus.

He received no sympathy from that direction. 'And you want the daughter for a wife? You are quite mad, you know that, don't you?'

So they rode in an uncommunicative group of four following the prints made by a horse whose hooves had a V-shape nick. It was simple tracking, because the unsuspecting courier had made no attempt to hide his passage over stony ground or through water.

It was only the next morning the three men became highly alert as smoke plumed high into the sky in a large cloud. Marcus, Crispus and Sellus exchanged meaningful looks and loosened their weapons. They changed their riding formation with Marcus in the lead, Crispus directly behind him, Macha in the middle, with Sellus bringing up the rear.

They rode at a walk, and very soon saw the smouldering remains of what had been a Roman fort. Now the men went on to very high alert as they halted and studied the ashes and bodies strewn everywhere. Some carrion birds rose, flapping heavily, their crops gorged on flesh; foxes scurried away. To one side, a small wolf pack watched their approach before backing off.

Crispus pointed. He and Marcus dismounted and strode over to a dying man while Macha and Sellus kept astride their horses and held the others' reins.

Marcus allowed the man to drink from his water bottle, then bent to listen as he struggled to explain what had happened. Crispus stood to one side, eyes everywhere, and with his long experience of many past battles, was able to work out exactly what had happened.

The soldier died, having virtually bled to death, and Marcus came back. 'It looks as if the whole of this frontier has gone up in a sheet of flame. But I don't think it will take long before a patrol from the other forts comes along. He said they were on partial alert because of smoke from ahead, which told them someone else had been attacked. What none of them expected though was the Britons' battle plan and the way they put it into force. They acted as one unit, controlled by one man instead of using their usual rabble-rousing tactics.'

Crispus considered. 'What you think we should do?'

Marcus never hesitated. 'We go on! We will deliver the mother to her daughter, and then we will have to play it by ear. There is quite a bit here that mystifies me,' he admitted.

Crispus nodded agreement. 'Someone has been copying our battle tactics and put them to very good use indeed,' he commented thoughtfully, and lifted one eyebrow questioningly at his friend.

Marcus pulled a face of agreement. 'We are both thinking of the same fighting female,' he said dryly, 'so all the more reason to ride on and follow these hoof prints! I am safe, they won't touch me, because of this crazy geasa, and somehow I don't think you'll be bothered either. As to the other two they are so obviously Britons they are safe!'

Crispus looked at Sellus and Macha. Both wore complete tribal dress and no one could have known Sellus had once been Roman. 'For the last few minutes I've felt a pair of eyes boring into my shoulders!' he said dryly. 'I think if we move forward, away from here, we shall soon have company!'

*   *   *

Kei nearly burst with excitement as he thundered up to Jodocca. 'Lady! Lady! Your mother is here!'

Jodocca braked her horse to a halt and looked disbelievingly at Kei. All this riding around had obviously become too much for him. He was going off his head.

'No, Lady, it's true!' he told her, then grinned from ear to ear. 'I knew your mother

242

was coming, but she swore me to secrecy. She wanted to surprise you!'

Surprise, Jodocca asked herself? She was thunderstruck. She swung her horse around as a group of the unharmed warriors thundered back to join her, wondering what was happening. With Kei in the lead, they went quickly back to the third fort and Jodocca braked, still bemused with shock. As she pulled her horse to a skidding halt she was further astounded to see Marcus Gaius. Even though in civilian clothes, he shrieked Roman, from his stance on the horse and general appearance.

The warriors whooped around in a circle, their blood hot with a battle victory and Jodocca saw the danger instantly.

'Halt, all of you!' she screeched and threw an appealing look at Cathus. He withdrew his javelin and charged at the nearest Britons. 'Back!' he bellowed.

'This group of four are my guests and are under my truce!' she yelled again and, slowly, the excited warriors stopped prancing and bellowing to see what was going to happen next. This really had turned into a splendid day.

Jodocca turned to her mother in complete bewilderment. 'But what are you doing— here?'

Macha had weighed up the dangerous situation in a flash. Deep down, she admired

Marcus Gaius and his friend Crispus, though she would never admit this. She looked pertly at her daughter.

'As you can't come to see me, I decided to come and see you and introduce you to your new stepfather!'

Jodocca sat mouth agape still hardly able to take it all in. So her mother had married again and a Roman too! So much for her lectures! She flashed a look at Sellus and noted how quietly he sat, with an imperturbable expression on a face still reasonably handsome. She also noticed how his right hand rested, just a little too casually, near a javelin. She turned her attention to Marcus Gaius. 'And what do you want?' she asked sarcastically.

Marcus did not deign to reply in words but let his eyes and his gaze speak for him. She gave an impatient shake of her head.

'It's him!' Crispus suddenly roared. 'The deserter!'

Cathus scowled and moved his horse nearer. Both Jodocca and Marcus acted simultaneously. Each bellowed a harsh 'No!' at the same time. They exchanged a quick glance again.

'You control yours and I'll handle mine!' Jodocca snapped.

Both Crispus and Cathus were coiled, and ready to strike at each other in mutual hatred. It would only need the wrong word, the wrong gesture, and they would be fighting to the death.

'There is a truce on now, and you two had better obey it,' Jodocca threatened.

'You can both stop preparing to act like stiff-legged dogs before a bone otherwise I'll join in with the lady!' Marcus roared in his best military voice.

'Traitorous dog!' Crispus spat.

'And you're still a loudmouth optio!' Cathus retorted with a snarl.

'Enough! Both of you!' Marcus roared again.

'I agree!' Jodocca grated. 'Now separate, and ride well apart. Llyn, keep an eye on these two for me, will you? Any trouble at all, and I give you and the rest of you men full permission to do some head cracking with some hard staves!'

Llyn and his fellow warriors were highly amused. Exactly what this was all about he had no idea, but they were delighted to follow any wishes of their highly respected lady.

Jodocca shook her head, flashed a look at Marcus, then moved over to ride with her mother while flashing a welcoming smile at the quiet Sellus.

That evening she sat with her mother, while Sellus tactfully left them alone to stroll down to where the two Romans were camped in solitary isolation watched over by rather bored guards, placed there by the chief.

245

Jodocca eyed her mother mischievously. 'All that talk about Romans, and now look what you've done. Married one, if you don't mind!'

Macha blushed. 'I plead guilty,' she said and grinned. 'What about you and—?'

Jodocca snorted. 'Him? I'm sick at the sight of him. I'm fed up with hearing his name mentioned. It was a bad day's work when he trod on my foot. He is the cause of my grandfather's death. And for that he'll pay. My geasa still holds good. I'll fight him and take him out once and for all!' she vowed hotly.

Macha hesitated now. She felt this was wrong in her bones but once her passionate daughter took the bit between her teeth nothing and no one could stop her. She looked around hopefully for an ally who might be able to reason with Jodocca. 'Aren't you forgetting one thing? He did his best by sending that note of warning!' she pointed out.

Jodocca simply sniffed disparagingly. They had been overheard as their voices had risen just a little too much and now they were the centre of everyone's attention.

Tristus chimed in first. 'Violence does not settle everything, Lady!' he pointed out softly.

Then it was the turn of Cathus. 'I am her official bodyguard. If there is any fighting to be done, then that's my job!' he said feelingly.

'Marcus Gaius did not hold that high rank for just being a handsome face. He is an extremely strong and talented warrior!'

Verica scowled at her husband. 'Jodocca was not made champion for nothing and look how she dealt with Riothamus. Anyhow, there is nothing you or anyone can do about it. The geasa was made in a public declaration, and anyone who does not follow such through becomes the contemptible fool of this island!'

Jodocca began to glower at them all. Only Verica was on her side. She resented her name being batted backwards and forwards like this.

Cathus bellowed, 'No!'

Chief Kersun intervened. 'Yes!' he declared coldly. 'We will not have outsiders, even adopted ones, dictate to us about our customs and way of life.'

'Here! Here!' Llyn cried. Like all of them he loved nothing better than a rip-roaring fight. Cathus realised an impasse had been reached. Only the storyteller was on his side. The rest of the tribal people broke into enthusiastic chattering at the promise of some remarkable future entertainment. That blood would be spilled was quite irrelevant.

Jodocca decided to end this line of conversation, once and for all. 'Anyhow, *who* is going to stop me?' she challenged in a cold voice and threw Cathus a very hard look.

Cathus was nobody's fool and he realised all were against him except the storyteller. He gave a forced shrug to his shoulders, turned and walked away. He would stop it all. How, he had no idea yet.

The next morning Jodocca took herself for a little walk in solitude and headed towards the small Roman camp. She nodded pleasantly enough to the watching guard, then strode towards the two Romans.

She eyed Marcus again, nearly letting herself be seduced by the aura of his masculinity. She quickly asked herself what did she really feel for him, deep down and in total honesty. If he were anyone else, and they had met under different circumstances, and his little finger had beckoned, she knew she would have followed him to the very end of Britain.

He watched her approach with sheer admiration, and not a little trepidation. Her eyes were hard, her face a mask, quite impossible to read. She gave a brief nudge to Crispus and spoke but one word. 'Alone!'

Marcus understood and flashed a warning look to his friend, who tactfully stood up, walked away to one of the sentries and, from force of habit, pushed him more erect and indicated he should hold his spear in a better position. Then he calmly walked around him, examining him from top to toe, halted in front of him and shook his head. The Briton stood flat-footed with amazement at this downright cheek, and simply didn't know what to do.

Jodocca kept her voice low. 'My geasa has to be settled once and for all, otherwise my name will stink!' she told him bluntly. 'Well?' she challenged, her stare brittle.

Marcus knew it would be impossible to flat-foot her like her mother. Other tactics were called for. 'Yes!' he drawled in a casual voice. 'It is time someone took you down a peg or two, and I'm just the man to do it!'

Jodocca could hardly believe her ears. 'Why you suffering, pigheaded, pompous bag of Roman wind—I'll make you change the tone of your voice before I'm finished with you!' she snapped. 'See that trail over there'—she nodded with her head so his companion could not understand—'follow that, it branches right, keep right and you'll come to a very large flat rock, overlooking a mountain river. There will be a good moon tonight and I will be there as near after midnight as I can make it. Javelins and daggers only, with a small shield, and just two of us. No spectators, no bodyguards, just me and you and our personal vendetta. Well?' she challenged, her eyes holding his unflinchingly.

Marcus felt his heart sink at the craziness of this situation, but he was an expert at keeping his emotions impassive behind a blank stare. 'Done!' he agreed, then could not help but wind her up a little. 'Stand by for the hiding of your life!' he promised evenly.

249

FIFTEEN

Jodocca knew she would have to use guile.
Macha and Sellus were in the guest hut as a
married couple so she had taken her sleeping
roll outside. She had cunningly chosen a place
well away from anyone else, and she settled
down, to all intents and purposes, composing
herself for sleep. Cathus was the great
problem, but he was with Verica who, at an
advanced stage of her pregnancy, liked him
near her all night.

Jodocca watched the moon rise and
wondered if this would be the last time she
would ever see the friendly light. She
examined her conscience closely and was
pleased to find that the thought of dying did
not disconcert at all. If she lived, the future
would be a lonely one because she knew now a
second marriage was not for her. She could
only envisage herself going down the years of
battle, until old wounds, the joint pains and
sheer age drove her into a corner of someone
else's hut—not really wanted by anyone.

How foolish had been her pipe dreams of
so many months ago. He would be a good
fighter, she might even have her work cut out
to best him, but she was confident in her
ability. She gently lifted her head to peep
around, but all was silent, there was no

movement anywhere. Moving very slowly, she slipped from her sleeping bag, then quickly stuffed it with some clothes and, standing, she studied it. A quick glance should reassure a distant watcher that she slept.

Slipping on some soft, very lightweight and silent shoes, she carefully picked up her javelin and small round shield, taking great care they should not knock against each other. One last glimpse around, and she padded onto the trail and started to walk briskly. It was easy to see where she was going with such excellent moonlight and she breathed lightly and easily. There was no need for her to work herself up, because already her blood was surging with anticipation.

She reached the edge of the platform rock and stood for a moment in the shadow carefully checking, then she saw him. He was standing in a casual pose looking up into the night sky, his face in silhouette, then some instinct warned him of her presence. He turned swiftly and for a big man moved quickly and lightly on his feet. This did not escape her as she stepped from the shadow and strolled almost nonchalantly onto the rocky platform.

He watched her approach very carefully. She did not so much walk as glide very lightly, her weight evenly balanced, all her movements completely controlled. It told him a lot as to what to expect, and he stepped forward to meet her.

Jodocca also scrutinised, his movements, the way *his* body was balanced, how his arms hung evenly with javelin in right hand and shield in left.

Neither of them wasted a word in speech. Two javelins darted forward in pecks to right and left, allowing each to assess the other. He was suddenly glad he had had the forethought to prime Crispus with more drink than was really good for him and that his friend now slept heavily, because Marcus suddenly realised this was not going to be a quick in and out affair.

For her part Jodocca was heartily glad of Verica's very advanced pregnancy, because it was hardly likely Cathus would leave her in the middle of the night. It flashed through her mind this was going to be the fight of all fights.

She opened up, dancing around him in a tight circle, with her javelin point stabbing at him, dodging the shield and first blood was soon hers as his left forearm opened up.

He was annoyed, but also totally disconcerted with her movements. He had guessed she would be quick, but her javelin became a blur. He tried to anticipate each thrust with his shield, then he opened up with some power blows intent on shattering her shield. Three of these landed, and she was forced to back pedal to the right, while her eyes opened with astonishment at the damage already done. Her shield had an ugly split at the top. One more power blow like that and it would split in half.

Her temper began to rise, and she increased the speed of her movements until he was forced to stand in one spot while she circled him, jabbing remorselessly.

It suddenly dawned upon him she really meant it! So his own temper elevated, and he concentrated on stripping away at her defensive shield.

It was Verica who woke Cathus for a drink, and he, knowing he would not get to sleep again easily, padded outside for a prowl. He saw the lady's sleeping bag, went to tiptoe past and had a sudden thought. He bent to examine, saw they were just old clothes and was immediately alert with horror. He stood a few seconds thinking rapidly, then broke into a run and bolted down the trail. It was obvious what was taking place right now, and there was only one possible site for a fight, which would give plenty of room for manoeuvring.

Crispus woke with a foul-tasting mouth, knowing he had drunk too much, and he staggered outside, shaking a bleary head when out of the darkness, a madly running Cathus crashed into him, and they both went flying.

Both men could only reel to their feet, but Cathus was the first to recover. 'She's slipped the camp!' he blurted. 'They're both involved in this stupid fight!'

Crispus gasped with shock, shook his head, regained his wits and looked at the red-faced Cathus. 'Where could they go?'

'I bet I know where! Follow me!'

They both raced like madmen, in and out of the moonlight and shadows with Cathus pounding in the lead and Crispus doing his best to keep up with him. The older man was suddenly conscious that he was nowhere near as fit as he used to be, his breath soon coming in very heavy rasps. They burst onto the extreme edge and halted for a few seconds, noting both the opponents flowing with blood although nothing appeared to be lethal.

This sudden, totally unexpected arrival shattered the fighters' concentration. Jodocca had darted sideways again to make a stab at her opponent's lower ribs. Marcus lifted his javelin and crashed it down on her shield in the most powerful blow he could wield.

Jodocca saw her shield split in two halves and drop at her feet. She nearly stumbled, gave a rapid little hop to one side, and badly miscalculated. She landed on the very rim of the platform and for two heartbeats knew exactly what was going to happen, but was powerless to do anything about it. She dropped her javelin, frantically flung out her arms to regain her balance, then she went over the edge, and started slithering, then rolling quite helplessly down through the scree. Finally, she crashed into the fast flowing mountain river and was near panic, because she was a poor swimmer. The river was powerful, the currents quite savage, and they tossed her helpless body backwards and forwards.

Marcus jumped forward in horror, watched for a few seconds, flung his shield and javelin aside, then launched himself after her, slithering and sliding also quite out of control. He crashed into the water, fought his way to the surface again, and frantically looked ahead, trying to see her body. He thought he saw a flash of long hair and struggled to head in that direction, his heart in his mouth.

The river began to cooperate a little, and with a huge effort his left hand reached out and grabbed one limp right arm. She was either out cold or already dead.

Cathus and Crispus raced to the edge of the platform and looked down with horror. The river was moving at a tremendous pace, white water boiling everywhere.

'Where does this go?' Crispus asked.

Cathus waved a hand vaguely to the left. 'A lot further down it broadens out, becomes shallow and quieter!'

Crispus gnawed his lip and with a white face, shook his head sorrowfully. 'I never thought he'd end up like this,' he said miserably. 'They can't possibly survive in this lot. They'll die from cold if nothing worse!'

Cathus knew he was only too right. Sentries had been left to watch over the Romans. Why hadn't they intervened? He knew why. Asleep! And he swore lustily.

Crispus eyed his belligerence, understanding in a flash. 'We must get others, follow the river and comb its banks in case—' and his words tailed off miserably.

'Come on then! Follow me and if you pass a sleeping sentry, kick his arse and I'll deal with them later!'

Both men spun around and pounded back the way they had come. Crispus had started to find his second wind now, and was able to keep up better as they burst into the small township. Cathus started roaring to attract everyone's attention.

Crispus stood by his side. 'Together on this one?'

Cathus threw him a very hard look. 'Of course. There may be a slight chance they are alive—' and he ran out of words, knowing he was lying in his teeth.

Crispus read him. 'Take it easy, soldier. We don't start to count the dead until we find the bodies!' he advised shrewdly.

Cathus was suddenly grateful to him. 'I'm glad you're here,' he said sincerely. 'You are right. Afterwards—becomes just afterwards!' he agreed, and each knew they had made a pact, a temporary truce of hostilities.

The river continued to rush downwards between rocks in a narrow part, not quite in full spate but with enormous power. It was beautifully clean, but lashing with cold, and Marcus knew he would have to do something. He held her close to his broad chest now, struggling to keep her nostrils in the air but spray was everywhere.

He could feel his strength beginning to disappear with this terrible cold. He strained with his eyes to see through the spray then held his breath. Could he manage it? He gulped and some more ice-cold water filled his mouth, then he took a deep breath and concentrated.

The sapling hung low over the river, and one branch dipped downwards invitingly. With a frantic grab, just as they were about to be swept underneath, he snatched it with one free hand and the branch bent sickeningly. It vibrated and whipped a little, but he tightened his hold and rather gingerly inched his way along with straining fingers. Very gradually, he hauled them both to the riverbank then scrabbling with his feet he found a purchase on gravel and stones and dragged them both from the water.

The water frothed angrily as if being cheated as he hauled them both on to a low-lying mossy bank. Jodocca suddenly opened her eyes, completely bemused, shuddering with the cold, wondering what on earth had happened.

Marcus looked upwards and narrowed his eyes. 'I can see a cave of some kind,' he gasped, and he supported her as she tried to struggle to her feet. 'We must get in there, get out of these wet clothes, otherwise we are both going to die.'

Digging deep for his last strength, they managed to scramble up and into a cave whose entrance was a deep fissure caused by some earth movement long ago. He staggered in first and was pleased to see that as the cave deepened, so it acquired a solid, tall roof.

Jodocca had slowly started to recover her wits. She leaned against the wall and looked around. Obviously, when the river was running very deep this cave partially flooded, because there was driftwood, twigs and branches, even dried leaves, littered around. She flopped down as her legs dithered from shock and strain. She had never felt so cold in her life but at least all the many javelin cuts on both of them had been washed very clean indeed.

She watched him, feeling useless and helpless. Marcus dived into a belt pouch and threw her a lopsided grin. 'All sensible soldiers at all times make sure they have the makings and the basic equipment for survival!'

He quickly gathered the crisp leaves into a

little pile, and with flint and tinder struck a spark very accurately. Within seconds, a tiny tendril of smoke showed. She made herself stand and hastily grabbed twigs, with him helping. Then, working together, they managed to collect other driftwood and had their fire. The smoke plumed upwards, vanishing through some ceiling crack for a chimney as it started to burn merrily.

'Strip!' he barked at her and pulled his own clothes off.

With another treasure from his pouch, he swiftly strung twine across the cave entrance and slung their sodden clothes on it. If they did nothing else, they could drip dry. Then he turned and took his time studying her nakedness and thoroughly approving. She was well formed with her muscles etched in sharp relief from constant exercise.

Jodocca gazed at his powerful masculinity and lifted one eyebrow eloquently. He was padded with large muscles, though here and there were old healed battle scars. Her previous husband had never stripped off like this, and as their eyes met she felt drawn to him. The fire's good warmth had already dispelled the violent shivering shudders when he half-lifted his right hand and beckoned. She never hesitated.

The cave floor was rocky and very hard, but neither of them felt this as they moved together instinctively and quite happily. He

259

was very experienced and took his time in playing on her nerves to draw her up to a high pitch before he moved into her. With enormous willpower, he again took his time and she was mewling like a tiny animal as he allowed himself to go towards his climax. Afterwards they lay happily before the fire, with his arms around her.

'So!' he murmured. 'That's taken a long time to achieve!'

Jodocca gave a chuckle. 'Hasn't it just!'

Marcus gave a deep sigh of pure satisfaction. 'Now let's get down to basic practicalities,' he began. 'I'm a civilian, and will never fight for Rome again. I have a good land grant in your home area and have had plans drawn up for my own villa. Once I can move in and settle I intend to breed horses. Fancy coming as my wife?'

Jodocca gave him a sad little smile. 'How can I? The authorities will want me for being a fighter against Rome.'

He shook his head. 'If you renounce fighting and war in general and also become my wife, you'll be perfectly safe,' he vowed. 'Aren't you fed up with fighting yet? Let your ridiculous geasa be the last one though we never did settle that properly. I think we'll have to call it a draw and let honour be satisfied with that. What do you say?'

Jodocca nestled closer into his arms, almost overwhelmed with an unusual relief. Here was the perfect escape for her and the chance to have peace and happiness like her mother and Verica. She had done more than her share for her people and for Britain, and deep down she had a nasty feeling the Romans were here to stay. This thought was unpalatable but her practical commonsense acknowledged that no matter how many Britons were flung into battle against the Romans, they had little chance facing the disciplined legions. It was true there would always be sporadic outbreaks and revolts but the reality of driving all the Romans back into the sea was fantasy. This acknowledgement was highly disagreeable, but she was honest enough to be completely realistic.

'I say yes to all,' she told him gently, 'but there may be culture clashes. You'll follow your Roman gods. I've followed the true Druids, so—!' and she halted, thinking rapidly. 'There is one among us who does nothing but talk about a man who was crucified. Strangely enough, the last time I saw my grandfather he predicted a new religion, and he drew a fish in the dust with his foot. Perhaps—?' and she stopped uncertainly now.

Marcus nodded. 'I've heard of them. They call themselves Christians but no matter how many are thrown to the lions or killed, they keep coming and coming! Let us talk to this storyteller of yours. Let us see what he can do for both of us,' he suggested.

Jodocca beamed a great smile up at him as they sat. 'My mother and her husband will no doubt travel back with us and she is going to want a villa as well!'

'So will Crispus. Once we settle down, he will want his own place near to us and then all he has to do is find himself a mate!'

Jodocca chuckled. 'At this rate, we will we make a little town!' she said prophetically. 'But—oh dear! I wonder what's happening above. I hope those two are not at each other's throats!'

Marcus shook his head with a grin. 'Your mother will be out of her head with worry. She has rather a strong character too, hasn't she? I don't think they would dare start anything personal while we are missing!'

Jodocca had to giggle. Macha on a matriarchal warpath was a frightening experience for anyone to think about besting.

'Cathus, your deserter will stay where he now is,' she told him.

'Best thing for him. Rome has a long memory—and so do the men. He will be as safe in this wild land as anywhere.'Then he moved and peered from the cave mouth. It must be about dawn. He found some wet wood and placed it on the fire. Immediately smoke eddied and wafted outwards now.

'Better get dressed even though our clothes are still wet. We'll have visitors in no time at all!' and he handed her a soggy tunic top. 'They'll have ideas anyhow as to what we've been doing. Let us at least appear presentable!' he grinned.

Jodocca stood suddenly, her features incredibly sad.

'What is it?' he asked with sharp concern . . . surely she had not changed her mind?

'I was thinking about my poor cousin. Everything has worked out so well for me, yet Caratacus—now placed in a slave gang!' and she shuddered.

He laughed and she turned, more than a little hurt. 'Forget slaves. Your cousin was a leader and Rome is not stupid. Far from it. He will be feted just *as* a leader and live the life of luxury with any of his family. It's true. He will never see Britain again because Rome knows all about leaders' presences calling fighters to arms again! There'll be no slave pens for him, so rest your mind on that point!'

Jodocca gave a huge sigh of genuine relief then a bellow reached them. 'Company coming!' she said dryly.

And within no time at all two ropes snaked down the hillside and, as if racing each other, Crispus and Cathus thudded down at the cave's entrance. The two bodyguards clambered in, looked at their respective charges, noted the large fire only just dying down, and also observed the twine, which had been strung in a strategic position for an obvious reason. They took it all in, then looked at each other knowingly.

Marcus and Jodocca exchanged an amused look. 'The first man who says the wrong word through any kind of deduction will go headfirst into that river!' Marcus threatened quickly.

'And I will see the second one follows!' Jodocca assured the two men.

Crispus and Cathus itched to pass comment, but managed to refrain. 'Everyone is on the path above. Your mother, Lady, is having umpteen fits of horror, and she has been very rough with both of us for letting you get away to fight!' Cathus said soberly.

Crispus chipped in with interest. 'Was there a winner?'

Jodocca and Marcus spoke together. 'No! It was a draw, and that satisfies both of us.'

Cathus said after a nod from Crispus, 'We'd better get you up the ropes, so that everyone can see you are sound of wind and limb, otherwise our lives are going to be hell.'

Jodocca grinned at Marcus. She could well imagine her mother's lashing tamper so they grasped hold of a rope each and within a short time reached the crowded path above. It seemed as if everyone possible was there, some mounted, and some on foot. There was a wild cheer as they appeared completely unhurt. When Marcus took her arm possessively and drew her to his side there were a few seconds of silence and then a volley of ribald comments.

Macha studied her daughter's expression, the glow of happiness in her eyes, the sincere smile on her face and the proud look of possession on the face of Marcus Gaius.

'He has her at last,' she hissed to Sellus. Now I wonder—?'

'Don't, wife,' Sellus said firmly. 'It's none of your business, this time!'

Tristus pushed his way forward and stood in front of Marcus Gaius. He looked long and hard into the Roman's eyes, then a gentle smile played across his features. He took the large hand of Marcus and reached over for that of Jodocca, then clasped both of them together in his two hands. 'Peace to both of you!'

The crowd watched this in silence, stilled by the genuine gesture, sensing this was something almost religious and sacred. Then again, they burst into spontaneous cheering and roars of approval.

Later on that evening, Marcus and Jodocca, Macha and Sellus, Tristus, Cathus and Verica with Crispus sat around an outdoors fire, and they all explained their plans, hopes and desires. Only Cathus and Verica would stay with the Silures and everyone else agreed this was wise. It was the breaking-up and the splitting in two of a little group of people who had endured so much together. But they still had Kei whom they decided would, twice a year, ride between the tribes carrying the news.

Marcus brought the evening to a close. They planned to ride back to the Dubonnii land, leaving at dawn. Tristus would accompany them. He had decided his life was better served with them and he also knew Jodocca regarded him in the same light as old Lud. 'I drink to all. For the last time. Death to our enemies!' he swore firmly, drained his tankard, and tossed it to one side. With Jodocca's arm in his, they walked away for sleep.

THE END

The Roman Occupation of Britain lasted for four centuries. Many soldiers who retired there swelled the ranks of a new race called the Romano British.

In a certain part of South Gloucestershire two farms have, for decades, turned up Roman relics. A survey was conducted and the sites of many villas were found with roads and other building areas. The archaeologists' deductions led them to pronounce that in this spot, at some time during those four hundred years, a thriving town had functioned and it was possibly even a regional capital.

It is reasonable therefore to suppose that people like Marcus and Jodocca, Sellus and Macha and Crispus put their roots down in this spot for their descendants later to become THE ROMANO BRITISH.